Christmas in
Cape May

D1546059

Also From Jennifer Probst

The Twist of Fate Series:
Meant to Be
So It Goes
Save the Best for Last

The Meet Me in Italy Series:
Our Italian Summer
The Secret Love Letters of Olivia Moretti

The Sunshine Sisters Series:
Love on Beach Avenue
Temptation on Ocean Drive
Forever in Cape May
Christmas in Cape May

The Stay Series:
The Start of Something Good
A Brand New Ending
All Roads Lead to You
Something Just Like This
Begin Again

The Billionaire Builders:
Everywhere and Every Way
Any Time, Any Place
All or Nothing At All
Somehow, Some Way

Searching for Series:
Searching for Someday
Searching for Perfect
Searching for Beautiful
Searching for Always
Searching for You
Searching For Mine

The Marriage to a Billionaire Series:
The Marriage Bargain

The Marriage Trap
The Marriage Mistake
The Marriage Merger
The Marriage Arrangement

Standalone:
The Charm of You
Summer Sins
Executive Seduction
Dante's Fire
The Grinch of Starlight Bend
Love Me Anyway
All For You

The Sex on the Beach Series:
Beyond Me
Chasing Me

The Steele Brother Series:
Catch Me
Play Me
Dare Me
Beg Me
Reveal Me

Christmas in Cape May

A Sunshine Sisters Novella

By Jennifer Probst

1001 DARK NIGHTS

PRESS

Christmas in Cape May
A Sunshine Sisters Novella
By Jennifer Probst

1001 Dark Nights

Copyright 2023 Triple J Publishing Inc
ISBN: 979-8-88542-043-3

Foreword: Copyright 2014 M. J. Rose

Published by 1001 Dark Nights Press, an imprint of Evil Eye Concepts, Incorporated

Acknowledgments from the Author

I love rescue dogs.

If you've read any of my books, you probably know this. The organizations that dedicate their lives to rescuing and helping animals in need humble me. I want to give a shout out to Animal Outreach in Cape May County, and the Animal Welfare Society who do this work in Cape May, NJ. Check out their beautiful animals for adoption or help by donating.

The fur gala and character of Bear are fictional. Also, the restaurant Vintage is one of my favorite haunts in Cape May for brunch—but I have never met the owner, and everything that takes place is completely fictional. As a writer, sometimes we create worlds we want to temporarily live in, and I decided spending time in the Vintage restaurant would be fun. Any mistakes or errors regarding this location are mine alone—but if you visit, I highly recommend the pancake charcuterie.

As always, special thanks to the 1001 Dark Nights team for allowing me to be part with my stories. Liz, MJ, Jillian, I love you all dearly.

One Thousand and One Dark Nights

Once upon a time, in the future…

*I was a student fascinated with stories and learning.
I studied philosophy, poetry, history, the occult, and
the art and science of love and magic. I had a vast
library at my father's home and collected thousands
of volumes of fantastic tales.*

*I learned all about ancient races and bygone
times. About myths and legends and dreams of all
people through the millennium. And the more I read
the stronger my imagination grew until I discovered
that I was able to travel into the stories… to actually
become part of them.*

*I wish I could say that I listened to my teacher
and respected my gift, as I ought to have. If I had, I
would not be telling you this tale now.
But I was foolhardy and confused, showing off
with bravery.*

*One afternoon, curious about the myth of the
Arabian Nights, I traveled back to ancient Persia to
see for myself if it was true that every day Shahryar
(Persian: شهريار, "king") married a new virgin, and then
sent yesterday's wife to be beheaded. It was written
and I had read that by the time he met Scheherazade,
the vizier's daughter, he'd killed one thousand
women.*

*Something went wrong with my efforts. I arrived
in the midst of the story and somehow exchanged
places with Scheherazade – a phenomena that had
never occurred before and that still to this day, I
cannot explain.*

*Now I am trapped in that ancient past. I have
taken on Scheherazade's life and the only way I can
protect myself and stay alive is to do what she did to
protect herself and stay alive.*

*Every night the King calls for me and listens as I spin tales.
And when the evening ends and dawn breaks, I stop at a
point that leaves him breathless and yearning for more.
And so the King spares my life for one more day, so that
he might hear the rest of my dark tale.*

*As soon as I finish a story... I begin a new
one... like the one that you, dear reader, have before
you now.*

Chapter One

God, she loved Christmas.

Devon Pratt looked around at her beloved flower shop and nodded with approval. She'd taken the entire day to pull out her boxes of décor and lovingly string lights and tinsel around the signs, counters and display cases. Now, the midafternoon gloom seemed more cheerful, like shining beams of light in all the dark corners and whisking away the demons. The holiday season gave her a sense of hope and peace, inspiring her to give back and treasure all the people she loved. Who didn't feel better gazing upon a shining Christmas tree with colored glass balls and a glowing star? Who didn't get excited over wrapped boxes with ribbon stacked together and peeking from prickly branches? It was all meant to lift someone's spirits and bestow a touch of magic.

That, and flowers of course.

She took stock of the new inventory of poinsettias in their bright red glory, along with pinecones, berries, and holly. Like the seasons, flowers followed the death and rebirth of Mother nature, and Devon found herself honored to be a witness. With every drooping petal there was a chance for a new awakening. Pruning was her favorite thing to do. Chopping away the excess to the bare core of a plant was similar to the grief and Phoenix rising of a human. Nothing stayed the same. Some looked at it as a curse.

Devon learned early to treat change as a blessing.

A silly grin curved her lips and she began humming as she hunted for Christmas carols. She was lucky enough not to have any big weddings to prep for, which was odd, but the past year had seen many brides and grooms wanting to wait for the new year. At least Alyssa—her part-time assistant—was able to go home and take some time off since Devon didn't need the extra help.

She'd miss out on the money—holiday weddings were fat with

profit—but Devon was looking forward to a break and focusing on the charity Fur Gala with Animal Welfare. She wanted to break all records since so many people struggled and gave up their pets. Under Devon's watch, every animal would get a safe home, and families would be able to afford them. The more focus she gave her favorite charity, the better everyone would be.

"Jingle Bell Rock" streamed from the speakers and she gave a jaunty little twist, singing off-key while she finished setting out the holiday village around the display of fir trees. She lit a candle and twisted red ribbon around the branches to create a pretty centerpiece. Walk-in clients were plentiful so she needed a surplus of arrangements in various budgets available.

The scents of balsam and peppermint drifted in the air. She worked till closing, enjoying the silence. She was used to it and had no fear. Sure, she dreamed of finding the perfect man who fit her, who GOT her quirks and issues and loved her anyway, but she wasn't about to waste her time bitching. Life was too short.

She had great friends, family, and a business she loved and had carefully built herself. She cultivated peace, happiness, and positivity. Negative energy was something she avoided at all costs. There wasn't enough sage in the world to cleanse some of the poison people liked to put out just so they wouldn't be alone in their misery.

But her floral shop catered to the hopeful.

Just the way she liked it.

Darkness settled over the small beach town of Cape May, but the white twinkling lights and carols and yummy scents beat it back.

She finished her centerpieces and began to pack up for the evening when the door flung open.

"Devon! Did you hear?"

She looked up at her friend, Jordan, who stared at her with wide dark eyes and flushed cheeks. "Let me guess. Vera is finally retiring and giving you the bridal shop."

Jordan gave an annoyed grunt. "Very funny. That would be when hell freezes over, and though it's cold out there, this place isn't hell. At least, not yet."

Devon grinned. Vera was a retired prima ballerina who ran the only bridal shop in town with an iron fist and a talent to please the pickiest of brides or grooms. Jordan had been working for her the past few years, and hoped to finally get her shot to buy it from Vera. "Sorry, couldn't resist. What's up?"

"Mac got called out of town. He won't be back for the Fur Gala."

Devon groaned. "No! The invites went out already, and we have no backup place to hold the event!" Her sudden selfishness hit her, making her pause. "Wait—is Mac okay? His family?"

"He's fine. His sister is pregnant and her husband is overseas. She asked Mac to come help her out for a while in Paris. He couldn't say no."

Devon relaxed. Good, she didn't have to feel guilty. "Well, I can't blame him—who could say no to Paris? Plus, he's the best brother ever so I can't be mad. But what are we going to do on such short notice?"

"No, that's what I'm here to tell you. Mac sent his cousin to run Vintage for the next two months. He'll do the fundraiser and everything."

"Oh, that's great." One look at her friend's mischievous gaze had Devon frowning. "What's the catch?"

"Babe, he's hot."

She blinked. "Who?"

"Mac's cousin! His name is Jameson—isn't that so sexy?" Jordan gave a delicious shiver. "And even better? He's single."

Devon fought the dread already forming in the pit of her stomach. There was simply nothing worse than a new single male coming into town, especially around the holidays. The busybodies came out in droves, proudly chirping about their fears over Devon's single status and how they didn't want to see her die alone and childless near the beach. Now, she'd have to deal with embarrassing gestures to try and set them up, which never worked. The last few men who'd come into town temporarily had not been even close to her match.

How could she be so happy with her life, but feel guilty for not doing what the town so badly wanted?

Settle down in a long-term relationship.

Devon shook her head hard. "No, Jordan. I'm done with matchmaking and gossip and humiliating attempts to set me up. He's here temporarily and I don't want to get involved. Do you understand?"

Jordan chewed her lip. "Sure."

Devon threw up her hands. "I mean it! Tell everyone to back off and let the poor guy run Vintage for his cousin without interference. Okay?"

"You haven't even met him yet! What if he's your soulmate?"

She spun on her heel and began closing up. "He's not. I'm grateful he'll be taking Mac's place so the animals don't suffer. I'll be nice and neighborly but that's it. And I demand your respect. You're my best friend for God's sake!"

"I know, but that's why I don't want you to leave any stone

uncovered. You're amazing, Dev. The funniest, sweetest person I know and I'm pissed no male in this town has scooped you up yet."

Her anger softened at the kind words. "Dammit, don't be nice or I can't be mad at you."

Jordan winked. "Then my plan worked. I gotta go, but maybe you should head over to Vintage and introduce yourself? I'm sure he'd love to chat about the Fur Gala."

"Maybe."

Jordan chuckled and gave her a quick hug, then walked out, her short blonde curls bouncing over her shoulders. They'd immediately bonded when Jordan first came to town, and Devon had to admit it had been nice having a single girlfriend to hang out with. They'd hit Atlantic City, Bethany Beach, and Wild Wood clubs till late at night, until Jordan ran into the love of her life at a bachelorette party—a curvy, fiery redhead named Sistine, who stole her designer purse on a dare and then stole Jordan's heart. Now, they were living together happily in Cape May and talking about getting married within the next few years.

Devon was thrilled but a tiny bit sad she'd lost her wing woman. Still, she adored Sistine and traded in one best friend for two. Not a bad bargain.

Maybe Jordan was right. She'd pop into Vintage tomorrow and welcome Jameson to town. It must be overwhelming to inherit a packed itinerary in a restaurant he wasn't familiar with. She'd offer her assistance and warn him of the town's shenanigans when it came to single males. They'd laugh about it and have some fun planning the Fur Gala.

Devon locked up the shop and headed home, whistling happily to "Jingle Bells."

Christmas was the best.

* * * *

God, he hated Christmas.

Jameson Franklin stared moodily at the restaurant he'd inherited for the next eight weeks and wondered how he'd manage. When Mac called to ask for the favor, Jameson didn't hesitate though he knew it'd be a challenge. Family helped family no matter what. He loved his cousin, but other than their shared passion for food, they were complete opposites.

His gaze took in the cheerful, homey type of décor that he normally avoided at all costs. Years working under one of the best French chefs had given Jameson a love for austerity, order, and restrained elegance. No dish or sauce came without a perfect pairing of red, white, or sparkling wine. He preferred small courses that led up to a finish, but without overwhelming the patrons with excessively sized dishes. There was a story to his menu at all times, and he took pride in running the Bordeaux Café in Manhattan. So far, he'd had no desire to open up his own restaurant, though he knew if he decided to, it would be a success. After a decade of living and studying the food industry, and being taught from the very best the culinary world could offer, Jameson knew all the factors to create a thriving business in a competitive industry.

He just hadn't felt the ambition or need to go on his own. Owning anything in this world meant not only responsibility but becoming limited in all options.

No, thank you.

He frowned at the limp garlands strung along the rafters of the dining room. The spray of white and colored lights littering the windows. The endless red flowers and cheap décor that made him feel like he'd stepped into one of those chain Christmas stores to bulk up on items for a house party. He'd completed a thorough investigation of the staff, menu, vibe, and setting, coming to one final conclusion.

Vintage was one hot mess.

He fought the urge to throw up his hands and squeak through, allowing Mac to keep his vision and habits, even though Jameson knew the man would be broke within the year. When he'd tentatively asked about profit margins, Mac had laughed it off, calling the restaurant the child of his heart. Besides serving an overabundance of high-quality food for reasonable prices, he seemed to open the doors to any type of not-for-profit party in the beach town, taking a hit on the expenses under the guise of charity. Vintage had been a BYOB place for years, and Mac only recently attained his liquor license—a perfect opportunity to increase profits. Instead, Jameson had almost screamed when he saw the wine inventory offered at cost, and no specialty cocktail menu where drinks were cranked up to fifteen dollars a pour.

Hadn't his cousin completed a business course?

Even worse? When he inquired why the BYOB sign was still out, Mac told him the customers still liked to bring their own champagne for brunch, and he allowed it.

He'd been struck mute in horror and unable to text his cousin back.

Mac cited large crowds, but it shouldn't be an element to boast about. From what he'd observed this past week, there were regulars who took advantage of low-balled prices, excellent food, and Mac's good heart.

Even the staff, as lovely as they seemed, had happily informed him of their revolving complicated schedules, telling him when they needed to leave or switch shifts as if he was running a college rather than a restaurant.

Jameson headed to the back, ignoring the slight throbbing of his temples. It was Friday and he anticipated a busy evening. After-work celebrations and family gatherings in preparation for the holidays had them fully booked. If only Mac took advantage of the customers' loyalty and tightened his ship, his cousin could make a killing.

Suddenly, he stilled as the thought hit him hard. His gut twisted with excitement. Maybe Jameson could help. Imagine if Mac returned home from caring for his sister and saw a brand-new Vintage? One with tasteful décor, higher prices, and a cocktail menu. He'd stop the bleeding and present his cousin with a thriving, profitable restaurant with a graceful nod of his head and a humble acknowledgement.

He had two months for the overhaul.

Mac was too entrenched with the locals, but Jameson didn't need to make friends here. He needed to run an efficient business. He could take the heat from Mac and transform the restaurant without worrying about being nice. He had nothing to prove. Who cares if they thought he was an asshole? They could grumble and whine about the changes, but in the long run, when Mac returned, he'd be making a ton more money and inherit a tightly run operation.

The challenge made the blood in his veins warm and his heart beat faster. It would be a wonderful lesson for him, too, and a way to figure out if he actually would like to run his own place. He'd help Mac out, and finally decide about his own future. A win/win with no casualties.

Jameson closed the door to the back office—a small drafty space with the basics, and whipped out his own laptop. He quickly made a list of top priorities to focus on during the next sixty days, checking the calendar to create a schedule that was ambitious but doable.

His finger tapped on the weekend of the 22nd which was blocked off in bright red.

Animal Welfare Fur Gala.

A frown creased his brow. How could Mac agree to such an event during the busiest weekend of the year? The restaurant would be blocked out for an entire day for prep, missing out on the lunch and dinner crowd.

He remembered the brief conversation with his cousin, and being told to give them whatever they needed.

For free.

A shudder shook through his body at the thought. He had no doubt Mac was being taken advantage of in the name of some unknown dogs. Sure, he believed animals should be safe and well-treated, but spring or summer would be a better time to push that agenda. Besides, how could he welcome dogs into the restaurant? It made no sense. He had the outdoor patio with heaters but what if it rained and they got cold? They'd trot inside with their shedding fur and bad breath and muddy paws into a place he was trying to transform.

No. He'd need to cancel it. He was sure the rescue organization would understand due to the circumstances of Mac leaving. The firehouse would be more appropriate, and he'd even offer to help with some of the food catering. Just as long as they didn't spend precious hours at Vintage drinking free booze and eating on his cousin's dime.

Satisfied with his decision, Jameson picked up his phone to break the news immediately.

Chapter Two

"Devon, the Fur Gala is cancelled."

She blinked at Jordan's shriek blasting into her ear and quickly switched to speaker mode since the shop was empty. "Wait, what do you mean? You said it was moving forward with Mac's cousin."

"That's what I thought, but I got a call from the shelter—Judith is frantic because she was told the dates wouldn't work any longer and Jameson suggested the event be moved to the fire hall."

"Wait—what? In two weeks? Invites have already gone out! Does Mac know about this?"

A hard breath huffed over the line. "No. Judith called him but the man was stressed because his sister ended up at the hospital and is now on bedrest. Judith can't bother him now when he put his cousin in charge. Oh, it gets worse."

Devon stared at the phone wide-eyed. "What else?"

"Judith has Covid. So basically, she's quarantined for the week and her staff has to deal with the fallout, and they have no time. It all blew up and I feel terrible. I want to help but I have a bunch of holiday weddings and fittings. Ugh, what is wrong with this guy? Doesn't he understand how important this gala is to the shelter?"

Devon couldn't help the amusement leaking through her voice. "You said he was hot and wanted to set me up."

"Not anymore! He's a grinch and shouldn't be here. What are we going to do?"

Devon clicked through the possible scenarios with the ease of an expert. As a florist who'd dealt with endless weddings, she'd seen hundreds of emergencies and learned to keep cool in hot-spot situations. Working with demanding brides and grooms trained her for excellent customer service and dealing with various challenging scenarios. "I'll talk to him. I meant to stop by but things got busy. Maybe if I explain the situation, he'll be reasonable. After all, he doesn't know the community here. I'm sure I can straighten it out."

"You are the best! Thanks, Devon, let me know what happens."

Devon smiled. Her friend had rescued three cats from the shelter and was passionate about the organization. Beach towns were notoriously hard to place pets and too many horror stories had occurred with tourists dumping their animals and fleeing. "You got it. I'll head over there now and take a lunch break."

Kissing noises came back at her. Devon laughed and hung up. It took her a few minutes to close up and put a sign on the door, then she headed out. The wind whipped at her long hair, the salty scent filling her nostrils. She hurried to her car even as she admired the roar of the ocean's fury crashing over the sand. Foamy tips of the waves hurled high and choppy under a gray cloudless sky. Even though she'd lived here for years, Devon always appreciated the thrill of living by the beach in a close community who cared about one another. She loved the hustle and bustle of the crowds during summer season for the raw energy and newness they brought in, but her favorite month was always December. Bed and breakfasts glowed with holiday lights, cafes created unique menus and drinks with cinnamon and pumpkin to warm the belly, and a low hum of excitement seemed to fill the air. Once January came, the place shut down, like flowering plants closed their blooms tight and slept. It was a time Devon loved to reflect on the past year, go inward, and enjoy that final blast of holiday gathering before hibernation.

Pumping up the heat, she drove to the Physick Estate, the famous Victorian house museum. The historical mansion was set near the tennis courts, courting a steady crowd throughout the year. Vintage was tucked behind the mansion, a quirky restaurant with flair and charm both tourists and locals loved. The long outdoor patio held large heaters to take advantage of milder evenings. Devon parked near the tennis courts and walked in, noting the patio was empty for the lunch crowd, but the main room was bustling.

She poked her head in and caught Trisha's eye, who immediately came over. "Hi, Dev." The young brunette was a college student known for her positive energy and sweet manner. Mac was flexible with her shifts due to her changing schedule, and Trish had been working at Vintage for the past two years. Today, Dev noticed there was a definite lack of bounce in her step and her gaze. "Can I get you a table? Take-out?"

Dev shook her head. "I want to see Mac's cousin. Jameson, right? Is he here?"

Trisha's lips pulled down. Devon didn't remember her ever making that dour expression. "Yeah, he's here. In the office."

"You okay, sweets? You look stressed."

Trisha sighed. "I just want Mac to come back. It's only been a short time and I'm miserable."

Concern flared. Trisha was beautiful and warm, which made her easy prey. "Wait—what's going on? Is he doing something I should know about?"

"Oh, God, no, nothing like that! He's just so different from Mac. He said no more changing my schedule, even though I have some family stuff coming up. Said the restaurant needed to be more efficient so no more flexible shifts."

"Did you explain Mac was okay with it?"

Trish nodded. "Yeah, but it didn't matter. Jameson said he was making major changes to Vintage. He called a big meeting with the staff. Marcus told me he wanted to quit because of the menu tweaks but he's sticking it out for Mac. I'm not sure what's going on, Dev."

A frown creased her brow. This seemed to be getting worse. "Can I go see him?"

Trisha jerked her head. "Go ahead, just make sure you knock first. I got yelled at for that. I better get back to my tables."

Her ponytail bobbed as she walked off. What kind of man did Mac sic on them all? Maybe it was a big misunderstanding and no one had let Jameson know how things worked around here? Either way, Dev had heard enough. She wasn't about to let him pick apart Mac's restaurant while he was dealing with a family crisis.

Squaring her shoulders, she headed to the back room and sharply knocked.

"Come in."

The voice should have warned her. It had that deep smoothness with a touch of arrogance, but she opened the door with a warm smile, figuring she'd kill him with charm. "Jameson?" she asked, cocking her head in inquiry. "Hi, I'm Devon Pratt. I run the local floral shop. Welcome to Cape May."

She waited for his response, keeping her smile at megawatt level.

The man peered over thick black framed glasses and pinned her with a cool, direct gaze. Her belly gave an odd little dip as she met those gray eyes that looked exactly like the day's sky. Cloudless, a bit stormy, and completely commanding.

Jordan was right. He was definitely good looking in a very hot-nerd way. He wore a dark, form-fitting suit that was way too formal, yet made him look perfectly at ease. A narrow red tie and shiny Italian loafers hinted he knew and enjoyed the power of a good accessory. Average height and weight, but broad shoulders filled out his jacket. His hair was slicked back from his face and the color of burnt caramel. Highly cut cheekbones set off his features with a touch of elegance, but his lips were lush and full, giving him an edge of sensuality that kept him from being too prudish looking. All of this was catalogued within seconds while she held her position.

"Ms. Pratt, it's nice to meet you, but I'm rather busy. Can I help you with something?"

She refused to stop smiling. "Please call me Devon. I'm here to help. I'm sure it's been quite overwhelming for you to step into such chaos, and with Mac being out of touch, I wanted to offer my assistance. I hope his sister is safely out of the hospital?"

A tiny crease furrowed his brow. "How did you know about Mac's sister?"

"Oh, everyone knows. News travels fast in this town."

He didn't look thrilled. In fact, he was studying her like she was a bug he was trying to analyze to see if it was worth keeping alive. "How archaic. Yes, she's safely at home resting."

"Good. I'm sure taking over the restaurant during the holidays has been a challenge. We all appreciate and support what you're doing for Mac."

He slowly blinked. "That's nice. But I've been fine. Everything is under control."

Devon shifted her feet. Her smile began to slip. "Well, I wanted to talk about the Fur Gala. My friend Jordan—she works at Vera's Bridal—said you were trying to get it moved to the firehouse."

"That's correct."

"I'm sure it seemed like a solid option but, unfortunately, it can't really be moved at this late date. Invites have been sent, and the firehouse is too small. That place is used more for birthday parties and anniversary celebrations."

"I'm sorry it won't work out. Let me know if you decide to hold it somewhere else. I informed Judith I'm happy to offer a smaller, set menu for the inconvenience. Nice to meet you."

He inclined his head as if to dismiss her.

Then turned back to his computer.

WTF?

She stared at him like a guppy, her smile long gone. Oh, this man was horrible. She'd hoped it was a misunderstanding, but now she was slowly realizing she was just dealing with an asshole.

Fine, then. She'd switch up her approach to something he'd better understand.

"Excuse me?"

He turned back at her sharp tone. "Yes?"

"I think we've had a tiny mishap of communication." This time, her smile was sharp and sharklike. She raised her chin a few notches to emit a strong energy to match his. "We'll need to hold the Fur Gala here at Vintage."

"That's impossible. I do apologize for the inconvenience, but I can't give up a Saturday of reservations at this point in the holiday season. It would financially harm Mac, and I'm sure that doesn't bother you or anyone else, but he's family and I'm looking out for his interest."

A hot wave of anger rushed through her. She shook her head hard to clear it. "I'm sure you don't realize as a newcomer, but Mac is both cared about and respected in this town. No one would ever take advantage of him. He's always sponsored the gala and I'm sure he would be devastated to learn his *family* deliberately ruined a beloved charity event he believes in."

Silence fell. Slowly, he refastened his gaze on her, but this time it held a flash of emotion that turned his eyes to a moody pale blue. Those full lips pursed as if he'd tasted something bad. "Are you a tattletale Ms. Pratt?"

Her jaw unhinged. Her voice grew a tiny bit shrill. "Excuse me?"

He waved his hand gracefully in the air. "Are you threatening to call Mac while he's focusing on helping his sister so you can spin a story that makes me look like the bad guy?"

A growl rose low in her throat. "I met you only five minutes ago. You *are* the bad guy."

A humorless smile touched his lips. "I intend to make some hard changes to help my cousin."

"I see. Do you have any experience in owning a restaurant or is this your opportunity to learn from a quick internship at all of our expense?"

He jerked back. Satisfaction flowed in her veins. Oh, she did not like him. There was nothing worse in her estimation than a yummily attractive man with a crappy personality. "I've run the Bordeaux Café in Manhattan for the past five years. I know how to create a profitable menu, establish an atmosphere that draws customers, and manage a large staff that offers competitive wages. I think I'm quite capable of knowing what Vintage needs even if it's about making difficult choices. Unfortunately, Mac leads with his heart."

"You can run a successful business with both. I'm sure you wouldn't understand that."

One brow lifted. "Perhaps the floral business allows for such indulgence. I can assure you the restaurant business does not."

And just like that, Devon lost her temper.

She took a few steps in and jabbed her finger in the air. "You wouldn't know how to handle a day at my shop, restaurant boy. And cancelling on a charity two weeks before the event is bad business in whatever way you want to look at it. I refuse to let you ruin this town's tradition because you want to line your pocket with a few extra bucks. I don't care what I have to do. You will honor the agreement and hold the gala here or I will make you sorely regret it."

The words shot and floated through the room like post-gunfire. A slight trembling shook her body from the depth of her emotions, and she dully noted it had been a long time since any individual—male or female—brought out her full ire. Devon braced herself for the fight of the century.

"Restaurant boy?"

The droll amusement only notched her temper higher. "I mean it. I will help you do this but you have a responsibility to keep your damn word."

The man had the audacity to lean back in his chair with ease and regard her under lashes that were too thick for a male. "And if I don't?"

Devon realized she'd make a bigger impression if she was like him.

Cold-hearted, methodical, and ruthless.

"I know people."

Interest piqued in those storm cloud eyes. "Mob?"

"No. Legal people. Wouldn't it be a shame to try and make productive changes and have to deal with customer complaints regarding the food? Or sanitary conditions?" She clucked her tongue. "Mac just got his liquor license. I bet you'd make a pretty penny selling your fancy Manhattan cocktails here. Wouldn't it be a shame if something happened to that liquor license?"

"You really like dogs, don't you?"

She narrowed her gaze and tried to figure him out. He was so damn…perplexing. Devon expected anger, or some other type of boorish behavior. Instead, he acted like he was royalty who refused to show weakness or emotion. Unfortunately, it only made her want to stir him up a bit to see where his limits were.

"Dogs are the bomb. They deserve a little happiness before being returned to their cages without a family for Christmas."

And then something amazing happened.

He laughed.

Sure, it was a chuckle, and not a full-blown chest laugh, but the sound ruffled her nerve endings and made her want to remember it so she could replay the scene later in her head. "Okay, flower girl. I'll give you what you want because I have limited time to deal with your threats but I have no time to structure this event. I'll serve local beer and wine. I'll offer up a limited menu based on my choices. That's it. You do everything else and there will be no interference with the lunch crowd. The event begins at six pm, and I serve till 4pm. That means, no early drop-offs or distractions for my staff."

She opened her mouth to say something but he kept going.

"And if I need anything, I plan to call you and only you. The moment you don't respond, I'm calling the whole thing off, and you can blame the dogs' broken hearts on your inability to follow through. Understood?"

"Flower girl?"

He grinned and her stomach did another weird flip. Something about those lips distracted her. "Tit for tat. Now, I need to get back to work."

This time, he turned around and began tapping at his keyboard.

She'd already been dismissed.

Head spinning, unable to come up with a proper retaliation, Devon left, wondering if she'd won the battle only to have lost the war.

Because dealing with that man for the next two weeks was going to be hell on Earth.

Chapter Three

Devon Pratt was a pain in the ass.

He stared at her as she filled up his inventory closet with decorations for the gala. The past few days he'd begun to regret his threat. He figured she wouldn't bother him until the week of the gala, but instead she'd taken his words to heart. The next day, she showed up to meet with the staff who volunteered to work the event to discuss set-up arrangements. Seems she wanted to tear apart the restaurant to allow plenty of room to display the dogs. Then it was demands for a finalized menu so she could create fancy place cards and deal with any allergy issues. She spoke of a doggy bar filled with toys and treats, which caused him a prickle of alarm. When he mentioned it, she announced with cold disdain it had been in the original plans agreed to with Mac.

Now, she was cluttering up his organized pantry with lights, mini trees, and endless sparkly things that dripped with holiday cheer.

The real problem?

His reaction to the woman's physical presence.

She…disturbed him.

Jameson studied her shapely form as she bent over, biting her lip and mumbling to herself. Her hip length, dark hair spilled down her back, stopping just above her denim clad rear. She reminded him of a forest sprite, with her large green-brown eyes, narrow face, and shiny straight hair. There was both a quiet stillness within her and a passionate animation that fascinated him. It seemed like one moment, she was studying him with intensity without speaking, and then her body sprung to life while she blasted him with a speech that edged his nerves.

Not to mention her voice. The sound evoked both music and smoke; lilting and husky until he wanted to take a step closer to hear more of it. Her laugh was just as sensual. Not that she'd laughed with him, but he'd overheard her with his staff, who all seemed to like her much better than him.

Trisha, one of the waitresses, interrupted his thoughts. "Mr. Franklin, I wanted to ask if I can have this Friday off. I'm working the morning shift but my mom called and she needs me to come home for the weekend."

He tamped down a flare of impatience. He'd just finished a meeting regarding shift changes and days off and was clear about his expectations. "I'm sorry, Trisha, but the schedule is done. You need to be here."

Her fawn-colored eyes widened with distress. "But Mr. Franklin, she's ill and needs help. My sister can't get there and she can't be alone."

Jameson shook his head. "I can't spare you. I'm sure there's someone who can be with her until your shift ends. We're missing Sheyann this week so there's no one to cover you."

Her lower lip trembled. "I know it's last minute but it's an emergency and I don't want to lose my job, but I have to see my mom. It's only breakfast—I'm sure Layla can handle it."

"One server cannot handle the entire restaurant."

"She needs to see her mother."

The blast of silk and sand echoed in his ears. Jameson turned to see Devon march over to stand beside Trisha. Outrage at her interrupting his conversation made him lose his words for a few seconds. "Excuse me?"

"Trisha's mom has an autoimmune disease and has been struggling this week. It's a family emergency. I'm sure something can be done to give her a morning shift off. What if Trisha was sick and couldn't come in? You'd manage, right?"

He clenched his jaw as Trisha leaned against Devon in gratitude. How'd he get to be the bad guy from trying to keep a restaurant running smoothly? "This isn't a sick day," he grated out. "If her mom needed help, I should have been informed by Monday so I could make proper arrangements. I have no one to cover the shift."

"What if you find someone to work?"

"Then she can have the time off."

"Fine. I'll do it."

He stared at her with shock along with Trisha. "You can't work here!"

"Why not? It's only a few hours for brunch."

"You have no experience as a server. I have no time to train you."

The woman actually gave a smug smile. "Yes, I do. I worked for years at a restaurant before I decided to open my flower shop. I can handle it."

He opened his mouth to reject her ridiculous offer, but Trisha emitted a cry and hugged Devon. "Thank you, thank you! I'm so grateful for this!"

"No problem, sweetheart. Go take care of your mom."

Tearfully, Trisha squeezed Devon one last time and raced away before Jameson could even speak.

He glared, caught between annoyance and a strange hit of arousal as she crossed her arms in front of her chest, raised her chin, and met his gaze head-on with sheer stubbornness. Trapped within those moss eyes, Jameson reminded himself she was an interloper trying to control his restaurant. "You had no right to interfere with me and my staff, flower girl."

"It's Christmas, restaurant boy. Are you always such a Scrooge?"

His voice iced. "Not everyone becomes a fool for a silly holiday."

She actually gasped. "Oh, my God! You really don't like Christmas?"

He wrinkled his nose with distaste. "It's overrated, commercial, and sets up everyone for a letdown. What's to like?"

"What about the trees? The lights? The presents? What about joy to the world and Christmas spirit?"

He practically sneered, warming up to his topic. "Christmas is an excuse to sell unneeded things to the population. To create doubt regarding your life, making one feel lonely, poor, needy, and empty."

Her jaw unhinged. He refused to acknowledge how cute she looked. Were those freckles on her nose? Somehow, they only emphasized her earthly beauty. Her pink lips parted. "Tell me how you really feel. Did you not get the video game you wanted when you were younger?"

He refused to smile. "No. I just think the world would be a better place if we didn't pin all hopes on a useless holiday."

Instead of joking, she cocked her head and narrowed her gaze. His gut tightened. "Something made you feel that way."

Oh, hell, no. He wasn't going there. "Must be nice to shut down your business on impulse. I should've been a florist."

That got her off topic. Steam practically rose from her head. "I'll have my delivery person watch the shop. Running a successful business means employing people you trust who will help when you call." Her sweet smile held poison. "I can't imagine anyone wanting to answer the phone for your call."

Damned if he had to smother a respectful laugh. Why was her sass so damn attractive? "Just make sure you pull your weight."

Her voice snapped. "Don't worry. You'll get your full use of me."

"Doubt it."

Her eyes widened at his impulsive retort. Immediately, his muscles locked down as arousal hit full force. The hidden meaning in those words suddenly crackled to life with possibility. Jameson refused to show emotion on his features. He refused to let her gain a hint of his interest. After all, it was just a shallow, passing attraction. She was beautiful and headstrong. He was a virile male who found her desirable.

But she was all wrong for him.

He pivoted on his heel. "See you Friday."

She didn't respond.

* * * *

Devon drove back to her shop and kept going over the scene with Scrooge.

Their relationship was...odd. She didn't like him. He bullied his staff, thought he could change Mac's restaurant to fit his own vision, and didn't believe in Christmas. Or dogs. He was cold and a bit arrogant.

Yet, she was aware of a simmering electricity underneath the surface as they traded barbs. Her body definitely recognized he was an attractive man. All that graceful polish and those gorgeously sculpted features were impossible to deny. The body under those classic suits seemed lean and muscled. Even more intriguing?

She'd caught the flash of a tattoo above his wrist, glimpsed as he shot his cuffs.

Jameson Franklin didn't seem interesting enough to get a tat. She wondered what it said or if it meant anything to him?

Devon wondered why she cared.

Shaking off her thoughts, she made a quick stop at the animal shelter to check in. The loss of Judith had thrown everyone into panic mode, and they were short staffed. Foot traffic was extremely low at her shop in the afternoon, so she texted Pandora to hang out an extra hour. Might as well see if she could help out.

The sound of sharp barking hit her ears at the same time the smell of disinfectant drifted to her nostrils. The animal shelter was small but mighty, housing an array of cats and dogs who desperately needed homes. Various kennels were set up, with personal touches to try and make the animals calm, including toys, bones, old blankets, and some pillows. A few couches were set up in the play room where they could socialize when the weather was bad.

Vishya waved at her from the front desk. The older man had moved to Cape May five years ago and been a life saver for Judith. He was retired, widowed, and thrilled to spend most of his days helping with the animals. He wore his usual bright floral shirt that strained a bit at the belly and faded jeans. Usually, his face was wreathed in a smile but today he looked a bit drawn and worried. "Hi Devon. Judith is still at home."

"I know, I figured I'd swing by to see if I can help out with anything."

Gratitude skittered across his features. "Appreciate it, but dealing with the gala is our number one priority. You're a savior."

She waved the comment away. "No, you guys do the real work. Is anything wrong or is it just general stress? You look worried."

He glanced back and rubbed his head. "Got a new dog and he's a challenge."

Sympathy flickered. "Biter? Aggressive?"

A short laugh escaped his lips. "Nope. The opposite. He's terrified of the other dogs and causing a ruckus. I feel so damn bad—I haven't seen a case like this in a while."

"Abused?"

"Probably, we don't know much. Found him abandoned out near Ocean Drive. Someone called it in saying a monster was sighted."

Devon frowned. "Monster? I don't get it."

"He's a bit...large. Was happy around people, a real love, but the moment he got here and saw other animals he went into panic mode. He can't stay at the shelter and all of our fosters are full. I need to find him a place ASAP with no other animals. At least, until I can figure things out for where to place him."

Her heart ached. She shifted back and forth on her feet. "Can I meet him? Maybe I can call around and find him a temporary home."

Vishya's dark eyes lit up. "I'd really appreciate it. I've exhausted all my contacts and so has the rest of the staff. His pic on social media has been met with crickets, not that I'm surprised. Come on, I'll show him to you quick."

Devon followed him back, and she greeted the other volunteers that had stopped in for the day to help with paperwork or cleaning the kennels. She passed a row of pups and the cat house until Vishya opened up the side door. "We're keeping him in here temporarily so he has no access to the others. But he can't stay in here—it's the meet and greet room."

Devon walked in, expecting a dog shaking in the corner.

Instead, the biggest dog she'd ever seen in her life cocked his head, gave her a hard three second stare, and rushed toward her.

"Bear, Bear—no, ah crap," Vishya yelled, trying to block the progress.

But nothing was stopping Bear from getting to her. In seconds, he'd knocked her back, tail wagging, massive head bumping against her in sheer affection. She caught her breath and her balance, and began laughing. "Does he think he's a Chihuahua?" she asked, petting him while he drooled all over her pants.

"Yep. Again, he's a people person. Pretty young, too, that's why he's so active. A real love but sloppy with manners."

"I'd say sloppy period." Her hand came away covered in dog hair, but between his wriggling butt, and large adoring eyes, in a few moments Devon was madly in love. His fur was chocolate brown with some scattered white streaks. "What breed is this?"

"English Mastiff. Hard to place. Very narrow niche of lovers for this breed."

"Why, his size?"

Vishya nodded. "Yep. Expensive as hell. Huge food bills, vet bills, and space issues. They shed a ton and drool consistently. Plus, their life span averages about six years. Most people don't want to get attached."

She rubbed his jowls, trying not to wince at the amount of fluid he leaked from his mouth, and wondered what would happen. Hopefully, a slew of calls and contacts would help her out and find Bear suitable space. "Aww, buddy, who wouldn't want you? You're a good boy."

He seemed to agree by slamming his head up and down on her knee. Devon laughed.

"We'll take any help we can get. If we can't find a place very soon, we're going to be in trouble. I've got a few emails out to other shelters so maybe that will work."

Bear bounded away to grab a giant stuffed snake, dragging him over with pride and shoving it in her hand. She tugged at it, expecting fierce resistance, but he was so gentle pulling it back between his massive teeth, Devon realized he was a gentle giant. "I'll work on it right away."

She spent some time playing and petting him, dreading when she had to leave. Finally, she dusted the hair off her clothes and stood up. "Okay, Bear, it was nice meeting you. You're a good boy."

She patted his head and inched back toward the door.

Bear sensed retreat and skirted around her, blocking the exit. Vishya laughed. "He does this whenever someone tries to leave. It's heartbreaking. He just wants company."

They tried to gently push him aside to open the door but Bear wouldn't budge.

Vishya firmed his voice. "Bear, no. Sit."

Bear blinked. Then whimpered.

Devon sighed. "You have to deal with this every time?"

"Yep. No one can give him the time he really needs for a new intake."

And then it happened. Knowing it was a terrible idea and she'd probably regret it, she uttered the damning words.

"I'll take him."

Vishya gasped. "Are you kidding me? You've never fostered a dog for us."

She winced. "I know." Devon didn't want to explain why. It sounded selfish and shallow and she wasn't ready for Vishya to know the truth. "But I'll do it until we find Bear a home. The holidays are a bad time for finding placement so this can buy us some time."

Bear stopped whimpering as if he understood her.

Within record time, Vishya set her up with food, a few toys, collar, leash, and made her sign some forms. She got in her Honda Civic with Bear taking up the entire back seat, drooling over her shoulder.

And just like that, Devon inherited a dog.

Chapter Four

Jameson stared in pure horror at the creature happily trotting in step next to his fill-in waitress. "What in hell's name is that?"

She barely acknowledged him as she whizzed by. The day was unseasonably warm, and he'd opened up the patio for brunch with the heaters full blast while the weak sun filtered through the drifting clouds. Reservations were full and he was excited to launch the tweaked brunch menu after convincing the chef to try something new. Seems the menu hadn't been updated in a long time. In Jameson's view, it wasn't a good way to run a restaurant. But instead of explaining it to Mac, he'd just show him the proof when his cousin returned.

If he could stay sane until then.

He raised his voice since he was being ignored. "Ms. Pratt—what do you think you're doing?"

Those gorgeous eyes regarded him like he was an irritation rather than her boss for the morning. "This is Bear. I inherited him until I can find a foster home so I'm tying him up here so he can watch the action and not be alone."

He almost choked. "Why didn't you keep him at home where he belongs? He's a monster. He'll scare away my customers."

She snorted. "He's a big baby and loves people. Just not other animals. I can't leave him alone because my place is tiny and he cries every time I walk into another room."

"He can't stay here. Go take him somewhere else."

She straightened up and regarded him with iciness. "He's traumatized and needs some help to heal. He was abandoned on the highway and some serious shit happened in his past. I'm asking you to find a shred of holiday spirit, okay? The customers will love him. Everyone loves dogs." She paused, narrowing her gaze. "Almost everyone."

A muttered curse escaped his lips. He studied the drooling, shedding Cujo in front of him, happily sitting on a blanket and giving Devon googly eyes. Of course, the beast was already in love with her. His insides squirmed at the image of the canine alone on the road and exposed to both the elements and other people's cruelty. He didn't hate dogs at all. They were just…a lot of responsibility.

The memory flashed before him and Jameson quickly shut it down. The past was past for a reason. He re-focused on the conversation. "Fine. But he better behave or he leaves. Understood?"

She rolled her eyes. "Sure."

His lips firmed at her obvious snark. "Put on your uniform and let's get going. You need to look over the new menu and specials."

With a last pat on the beast's head, she sauntered over. "Why'd you change the menu? Everyone loved it."

"Change equals growth. The place needs freshening up and I'm happy to do it."

"How'd you get Marcus to go along with you?"

The lie about the chef eased from his lips. "He was excited to do something different."

Her snort said she knew the truth but he refused to spar with her. She finally gave up on arguing and left to change. Jameson glanced at the dog, who suddenly looked fearful of being without his mistress. Those big dark eyes fastened onto him and the beast whimpered.

"Ugh, she'll be back soon. Just chill."

Another moan. Sweat broke out on his skin. He couldn't deal with this now. He was going to kill Devon. Having her fill in wasn't worth this emotional hostage situation.

Thankfully, she came right out in a snug black t-shirt and skirt. He tried not to stare and freak her out. Her long hair was braided and swinging down her back. The uniform was simple—Mac had refused to make the staff dress universally so he'd taken care of that—but the fabric clung perfectly to all her curves, showing off muscled calves and an ass that made his mouth water. Jameson had a sudden impulse to close the distance, tip that stubborn chin up, and press his lips against hers. He wondered what she'd taste like.

Holy hell, he needed to stop. The woman was irritating and stubborn. He preferred his dates to be amenable, gentle-natured, and easy to please. Working in the restaurant business was too stressful, and he didn't want to waste his time fighting over why he was so busy or refused to commit. He had a feeling Devon wouldn't agree to his terms. She'd probably insist on her own.

"I don't like these uniforms. They're boring and too tight. I don't like skirts."

Jameson grabbed onto his patience. "It's a traditional uniform and you're the only one who's complained." He refused to share that the rest of the staff had said the same, asking for red and pink and yellow instead of black. And shorts—none of the women liked the skirts.

"Just trying to help."

He shook his head to clear it and handed her a menu. "Memorize it. Here's the table chart. Layla is hostessing so she'll help with any questions."

He pivoted on his heel.

"Wait! Where's the pancake charcuterie board?"

"I got rid of it. Do you know it's been on the menu since the place opened? Too basic."

He kept walking but she trotted after him. "Wait! That's everyone's favorite. You never take away a signature dish."

He tamped down an impatient sigh. "Anyone can get pancakes, bacon, and sausage."

"Not two kinds of bacon with fresh fruit and Nutella!"

He lifted a brow. "You can purchase each of those ingredients at any supermarket. Vintage is better than that."

"No one wants a fancy lobster taco that costs fifty dollars. And what's up with the cocktail menu? There's a big ass sign saying all BYOB requests will be denied, and you're pushing blood orange mimosas and jalapeno margaritas? People want to bring their own alcohol to save money. Or buy a Cape May White and call it a day."

He gave her a good hard glare. "Everyone loves lobster and a specialty cocktail. We're at the beach. It's expected."

"Breakfast platters and BYOB is expected at Vintage. It was built on traditional favorites. You're ruining it."

He leaned in. "I guarantee the lobster breakfast tacos and drinks will be a hit."

"And I guarantee your customers will complain about the pancakes."

"Wanna bet?"

He didn't know what made him say it. Maybe the smug expression on her beautiful face, or the way she was constantly trying to challenge him on anything he did. All of his testosterone exploded and he only knew he wanted to win. Her moss green eyes lit up with interest. "What do you mean?"

He shrugged. "We see what the guests prefer."

The woman actually rubbed her hands together with glee. "This is awesome! What do I get when I win?"

"I've been in the restaurant industry for years," he said almost gently. "You should be asking what I get when I win."

"You may know the industry, but you don't know your customer, restaurant boy."

Jameson tried to keep civil. "When I win, you stop giving me a hard time about everything. No more questioning my decisions. I will expect not only your full support, but for you to spread the word about town that Vintage has never been better under my direction."

He tried not to grin at her horrified expression. "I have to lie?"

"No, you have to tell the truth."

She ignored him and gave a suffering sigh. "Fine. Thank goodness, I won't lose."

"Keep dreaming, flower girl." He began to walk away but her lilting, velvety voice stroked his ears and made him still.

"When I win, you take Bear."

Slowly, he cranked his head around. "Excuse me?"

A big ass grin curved her lips. Hands crossed in front of her chest, she practically vibrated with glee. "You heard me. You foster Bear until I can find a home for him."

He blinked. "I'm in Mac's house. That's impossible."

"No, it's not. Mac always helps out with fostering animals. In fact, six months ago, he fostered a golden retriever for a few weeks and loved it. He'll be fully on board."

The idea was so impossible, he refused to consider it. There was no way he'd be stuck with a slobbering, shedding, giant whining baby who refused to be left alone. He needed his quiet and peace when he left the restaurant. No, it would never happen.

He believed in himself and his skills.

It took all of his expertise not to show his concern. "Fine. It won't matter anyway."

She began laughing, and Jameson tried not to shudder. The sound reminded him of victory.

He hurried off with the echoes in his ears.

* * * *

"Hi, folks. Welcome to Vintage. My name is Devon. What can I get you?"

The couple glanced at each other warily. The man wore a reindeer Christmas sweater and a red ball cap that said Let the Festivus Begin! His wife was dressed in black pants, a green blouse, and a brightly colored scarf stitched with wreaths. Her smart gray bob curved under her chin and showed off her dangly silver earrings. They looked like an upper-class couple in for the weekend to see the holiday lights and enjoy the beach town. "Well, we must've been mistaken about the bar. We brought our own champagne but I see they're serving cocktails?" the woman asked.

She swallowed her grin. This was the fourth table disappointed they couldn't drink the bottle of booze they brought. "That's right, we got our liquor license. There's a delicious blood orange mimosa you may enjoy."

A frown knit the woman's brow. "I guess. Okay."

The man gave a smile that deepened the creases around his eyes. "I'll just have pineapple juice, please. Oh, and can we get the pancake charcuterie platter? We'll split it."

Now, she had to try hard not to giggle. The first hour was filled with confused repeat customers who couldn't understand why the pancakes were gone and two had mentioned the high price of the lobster tacos. "I'm sorry, that's no longer on the menu."

The gentleman looked upset. "But it's our favorite. This is the second time we've been here. Can the chef prepare it anyway?"

"I'm very sorry but we can only do what's on the menu. May I suggest the lobster tacos? It's a new special and quite popular."

The woman's face fell. "Oh. Well, I guess. What do you think, Martin?"

"Did they take away the flatbread too?" he asked with a touch of irritation.

"No, that's still here."

"Fine, I'll have that. Thank you."

She smiled and walked away, stopping by Bear to check on him. The family at the table was pointing and smiling at him, while the little girl with pigtails called him a magical creature from the book she was reading. Bear loved the attention, giving them a goofy, drooly grin and cocking his gigantic ears as if he knew they were talking about him.

That table had wanted the pancakes, too.

Devon checked in with Layla. "Table four asked for the charcuterie board," she whispered.

Layla noted it on the pad of paper. "Got it. He's going to be pissed."

"Probably. By the way, what do you think of the uniforms?"

She wrinkled her nose. "Hate 'em. I asked for pink. The guys wanted it, too."

"I hear you."

"When is Mac coming back?"

Devon patted Layla on the shoulder. "When his sister is ready to let him go. Hang in."

She kept careful tally of the orders and comments, while keeping an eye on Jameson. He seemed to be doing his own survey, stopping at each of the tables before they left to chat, looking distinguished in a black suit with a silver blue tie. She wondered what his body looked like underneath all those designer fabrics. She wondered if he had tats anywhere else. She wondered if those lips could dazzle in bed as much as they pricked in speech. She wondered—

No. She would not think about him like that. Since the moment he got into town, he'd tried to wrestle control of Vintage, cancel the Fur Gala, force her to work for him, and challenge her to a bet he believed was impossible for her to win. It was rare her body craved someone her mind didn't. Her past relationships had always been in sync with no hesitation regarding what she wanted. This odd interest in Jameson had thrown her off.

Devon reminded herself she just needed to teach him a good old-fashioned lesson. If she won the bet, he'd be taken down a notch, and maybe it would slow down his roll with trying to change Vintage.

The rest of her shift flew by, and finally they reached the dead zone between brunch and dinner. Her feet and arms ached but a sense of satisfaction buzzed through her. Another reminder of how her energy surged when she was helping people.

She pressed her lips together at Jameson's usual frown. Seems like he didn't share the same buzz. Why would he have gone into the restaurant industry if he didn't like customer service? Devon imagined he'd be better suited to research, where he was contained in a back room and could rule his own world, on his terms.

He strolled toward her with a purpose that made her wonder what it would be like once he claimed a woman. Was he possessive? Direct? Would he approach seduction as a goal to be met, or did he ever let go during the journey? He stopped a few inches from her and she caught his scent—clean and crisp, with a hint of lemon. Those cool pewter colored eyes flared with a hint of smoke and threw her a tiny bit off balance. "Did you cajole them?"

She blinked. "Cajole who?"

He cut a hand through the air. "The customers. Did you cajole them to order the charcuterie so you could say it's off the menu?"

Oh, this was priceless. His face tightened with annoyance. "Cajole, huh?" she drawled. "Bringing out the big words, restaurant boy?"

"No, I just happen to read."

She ignored his biting comment. "Are you pissed off you lost the bet and looking for excuses?"

He practically spluttered with outrage. "I don't welch on bets, flower girl. But I wouldn't put it past you to flirt to get your way."

This time, she spluttered. "Flirt? With who? There weren't even single men here for brunch!"

He snorted. "You don't need a single man to flirt. You do it with everyone."

"That's called being nice. Maybe you should try it sometime. You may get what you want."

They glared at each other. His nostrils flared. She watched with fascination as he got himself back under control, and the smoke in his eyes turned to burnt charcoal. "Bring the beast to Mac's place tonight."

Devon knew her smile dazzled. She couldn't help leaning close and lowering her voice to a sexy whisper. "Pleasure doing business with you."

She didn't wait to relish his reaction. Just spun on her heel and walked away.

Her encounters with Jameson Franklin should not be this much fun.

Chapter Five

Jameson wondered why he was looking forward to seeing her.

He paced the living room in moody silence and waited for her arrival. He couldn't understand how this slip of a woman got under his skin and stayed there. And why had he made that ridiculous bet? He knew the rules. Never wager unless the odds were ninety percent or higher. Had he been that confident in the new menu? Honestly, he'd been taught better than this. When bringing anything new to customers, there was always a transitional period where people fought change. Even if the place wasn't good, it was what they knew.

He'd tried to create excellence too quickly, then got too cocky. But it was hard not to try and show Devon he knew what he was doing. She made him question his natural leadership skills, and simply put?

It pissed him off.

After all, she sold flowers, which must be the easiest job on the planet. Having her challenge each of his decisions while trying to deny his attraction was difficult. He was a master at separating his emotions and ignoring the messy parts of himself he refused to indulge. Devon pushed at his boundaries. It was hard not to stare at her while she flitted around Vintage in that tight black skirt.

The exact uniform he'd insisted on.

But it was more than her gorgeous body. He'd watched her interact with the customers with such a natural warm energy, everyone wanted to be part of her orbit. The way she threw her head back and laughed without restraint. How she seemed to create an intimacy with each person within such a short time. He'd watched professional waitstaff try to emanate those qualities and fail because it wasn't a core part of them.

Devon naturally exuded radiance with every person around her.

Except him.

The only thing he seemed to coax was sharp-tongued retorts.

On cue, the bell rang. He drew in a breath and opened the door.

She wore clingy yoga pants, a faded peach t-shirt that said BLOOM, and a big ass grin. The dog pressed against her leg, panting. Drools of saliva pooled around his massive paw. "Bear, meet your new daddy."

He almost choked. "Very funny. This has an expired timeline, you know. I can't keep a dog with my schedule."

"No worries, you can bring him pretty much everywhere."

He shook his head as she stepped past and unclipped Bear's leash. The monster immediately prowled around the space, ears perked up, fur flying with each step. "I can't believe Mac agreed to this. He has a pretty nice place that's going to be ruined."

His cousin had bought a generous sized house in North Cape May, about ten minutes from town. White with turquoise shudders, it was located on a prized corner lot a few blocks from the bay. Jameson liked the fenced yard and front porch for enjoying outdoors, and the large kitchen outfitted with all updated equipment. He wasn't as thrilled with the eclectic furnishings, and endless knickknacks his cousin loved to collect. There seemed to be no single theme, just a mishmash of beachy furnishings in various bright colors. Teak tables, wicker rockers, and braided rugs covered a birch wood colored floor. Throw pillows painted with seagulls scattered atop worn navy blue sofa cushions. Happy painted signs declaring Beach Home and Summer Vibes blended with some badass canvases consisting of a half-naked woman poised on the end of a cliff. The brushstrokes were bold and moody and Jameson found himself drawn to the artwork, studying them for long periods of time.

He wondered if Mac did weed, or if he was just naturally quirky with his taste.

Devon dragged in a large tote bag and set it on the floor. "I brought his food, some bowls, treats, and toys. Mac has a few large dog beds in the attic he keeps on hand." Her ponytail swung as she looked around the house. "How are you settling in here? This doesn't seem like your normal style."

He tried not to take offense and cocked his head curiously. "What do you think my style is?"

Her bottom lip quirked in a half smile. "I'm guessing modern. Clean lines. Minimal furniture."

He hated that she was right. His loft apartment was stark black and white with metal sculptures and custom-made light fixtures with an industrial flare. He loved space and breath in his architecture though he was also comfortable in a tiny cramped pantry or kitchen. "Correct. And I would guess your place is filled with flowers?"

That got her to laugh. "Correct. Though I keep the good stuff for my shop since I'm there all day. My place is above the store so it's an easy commute."

He wanted to see her personal space. Imagined it bright and cheerful with just a hint of edginess. "Have you always lived in Cape May?" he asked.

Bear pushed his head around the corner, checking to make sure they hadn't moved. His giant tail whacked against the wall in doggy delight, and then he disappeared again.

"No, I'm originally from New York."

He lifted a brow. "Really? What part?"

"Soho." A smile touched her lips like she was caught in a memory. "I did the fast lane for a while. Held two jobs, did yoga at six am every morning, and brunch every Sunday. One weekend I went to a friend's wedding in Cape May and when I crossed the bridge, my entire soul vibrated."

"You'd never been before?"

She shook her head. "I wasn't really a beach person. Or so I thought. That weekend changed everything. I walked into the water and watched dolphins play in the waves and I cried."

Jameson moved closer, fascinated by the softening of her features, the relaxed curve of her lush lips, the sparkle in her eyes. "Why?"

A tiny laugh escaped. "Because I hadn't known I was unhappy until that exact moment. I quit my jobs and moved here within the month."

He studied her angular chin and stubborn jaw and the glow of her skin. "You're very brave."

Her gaze swung to his, obviously startled. "I figured you'd say impulsive or silly."

"No. Too many people ignore the signs of what they're supposed to do or where they're supposed to be. We feel stuck but are too fearful to make a change. You're a bit of a warrior, flower girl."

The space between them warmed and electrified. He sucked in his breath at the sudden sexual chemistry crackling between them, pulling him closer. His nostrils flared as he caught her scent. Vanilla and currant. Earthy. Sexy.

He liked the tiny catch of sound she made in her throat. She felt it too, and though it made no sense, Jameson decided he really, really wanted to kiss her. He needed to know how she tasted and if she'd melt under his touch or bring her own sensual sting to the kiss.

He reached out.

Bear barreled in and skid between them. He wrinkled his nose at the scent of wet dog. "Why is his snout dripping wet? I don't have any water bowls out."

Devon sighed. "Toilet bowl. You need to keep the lids down."

"Yuk. He's so…messy."

"Love is not supposed to be neat and tidy, restaurant boy."

Her words struck something within him and all those safe barriers he'd erected began to shake. Clenching his jaw, he fought it back and everything steadied. The mood was broken so he grabbed the bag and brought it into the kitchen, ignoring the funny look she gave him, almost as if she'd discovered his secrets.

Bear followed, sticking his wet nose into the bag. His furball body swung around and a crash echoed in the air.

Devon winced. "Yeah, you're gonna need to clear off these table tops. He can't help his size and can't judge when he'll knock something down."

Jameson glowered. "Do you see all the junk in this place Mac collected? Why do I have to change my setting to accommodate a dog?"

She gave him a firm stare. "Because he's a baby and your responsibility."

"He's a menace and a short-time visitor."

"Bear's had a hard time out there. Haven't you just wanted to feel safe?"

He jerked back and turned away. The words hit its mark. "Yeah."

"When?"

Her question thundered in his ears. The memory resurfaced and taunted. He practically squeezed his eyes shut to avoid all off it. "Before. Fine, I'll clean up in here."

"I'll help. Grab a big bag or something we can pack the stuff in."

Muttering under his breath about her bossiness, he retrieved a tote and began removing the knickknacks from the tables. Bear sat and watched them happily.

"Want a beer or glass of wine?" he asked.

She squinted at him, which made him laugh. "What's so funny?"

"You're acting like I'm about to poison you instead of offering you a drink."

She grinned. "Sorry, you've been a bit prickly. Sure. I'll take a beer."

"Cape May White, good?"

"Perfect." He popped open two, grabbed glasses from the freezer, and poured.

"Thanks." She took a sip, sighing in happiness at the chilled brew, not seeming bothered by the foam covering her lips. "Damn, that's good."

"A frosty glass makes all the difference."

"I'm sure next up will be a temperature-controlled wine fridge for Vintage," she teased.

He grunted. It had definitely been on his list as a necessary investment. "I'm not prickly. I'm a bit of a perfectionist when it comes to business. It's probably different from the way you run a flower shop."

Her smile was wiped away. Jameson mourned it. "That's the third time you made some crack about me being a florist. You have no clue what I handle."

"Tell me. I'm curious."

Her brows snapped into a fierce frown. She looked adorably grumpy with that expression and he had to fight his instinct to reach for her. His emotions were all over the place with this woman. He'd never reacted to someone like this—laughter, irritation, sexual attraction. It was like a giant ball of mess.

Devon took another sip of beer as if to fortify herself. "I get up at six am so I can prep the shop, take care of the flowers, and deal with ordering supplies. I get ready for deliveries and plot out the schedule. Depending on what event I'm working on, I may need to travel to get some rare blooms. I have consults during the day since I do endless events—from school functions, weddings, holidays, birthdays, beach picnics, etc. I also have regular customers who come and go daily, including local hotels and restaurants. Weekends are mainly spent setting up for events, which you should know, can exist within complete chaos."

He nodded. "Yeah, I can relate. Bad tempered chefs, ruined food, demanding customers, food allergies. I've seen it all."

"Exactly. Flowers are the crux of many celebrations. Making sure I have quality blooms on hand is a big deal. It's also extremely creative. Many brides and grooms have no idea what they want. They'll come in with odd demands or pictures, and it's up to me to pull it all together and coordinate so everyone is happy. I work my ass off every damn day. I'm not tiptoeing through the tulips with no stress, you know."

He grinned and threw up his hands. "I get it. Honestly, I never really thought of flowers on the back end. I just see the finished product."

"Just like a restaurant."

"Yes." She seemed satisfied with his reaction and took another sip of beer. He craved more from her, so he focused on his task of tidying up so he could hide his deep interest. "Why flowers and why own your own business?"

Devon placed a snow globe with a beach Santa in the tote, then absently patted Bear's head. "My parents had a massive garden. We lived in upstate New York, near New Paltz, in this old farmhouse. Every day, mom would pick an arrangement of fresh flowers and put them all over the house. I woke up every morning to the scents of roses, hydrangeas, and lavender. She taught me the balance of delicacy and strength, and all the tricks to keep them healthy." A short laugh escaped her lips. "I learned most lessons from my life by being around flowers."

He dropped the bag, no longer caring if he looked hungry for more. Her musical voice wove a spell around him, urging him closer. His fingers itched to touch her cheek, slide his palm to the nape of her neck, and tilt her head back. "Like what?"

Her eyes widened. She took a few moments to study him, as if testing to see if he was teasing her. "Lessons? Pruning is one. Sometimes, you need to chop away parts of yourself to be able to grow stronger. Learn to trust the strength of the flower to grow back when the time is right."

"What if your timing is wrong? If you prune too early or too late?"

Her lips pursed in thought. "Then you learn from the mistake and get it right the next time. You learn what the flower needs and forgive yourself. Then try again."

His head spun. There was so much more going on within this conversation. He'd never touched deeper topics with a woman. He was great at banter, flirting, and sex. He was a master at break-ups, taking the blame for his insane schedule and inability to commit long-term. Jameson never took the time to really dig into the why—he went with instinct and kept his head down, plowing through his days and his life with little reflection.

Devon made him want to poke around. Learn what was beneath her gorgeous exterior and find what made her so uniquely her. Ask himself some questions he'd never considered.

In that moment, he realized this woman was dangerous.

"What made you want to run a restaurant?" she asked, turning the conversation around. He avoided her gaze, needing to sort through his sudden drama.

"I like being around food."

She laughed at that, and a reluctant grin tugged his lips. "Elaborate," she teased.

Usually, he gave the easy answer. He'd grown up with an appreciation for good food, gotten his first job at a local restaurant as a bus boy, and fell into the career. But he wanted to share a bit more with Devon. "There's an order within chaos," he slowly said, trying to find the right words. She tilted her head, her focus fully intent on him. "I get high off the rush of the kitchen and the urgency to get the food on the plate in the proper way, in the proper time. The buzz of energy is so intense everyone is vibrating at such a high level. And then you walk through the doors to the main dining room and there's this peaceful type of organization amidst the frenzy of seating everyone, or getting their drinks and meals to the tables. It's both creative and risky. I found my favorite part was trying to control the logistics in order to minimize the unknown. Being in the thick of a Friday evening rush and pulling it off gives me satisfaction."

She nodded slowly, as if she understood the feelings beneath his explanation. "Order within chaos," she murmured. "How beautifully said."

He shifted his feet in discomfort. "Plus, the money is really good."

Her laugh caressed his ears. "I'm sure it is." She finished her beer in one long swallow and handed him the full tote. "All set. I better get going."

She bent over and whispered something in Bear's ear. The dog panted, shoving his body against her. He noticed she was covered in dog hair but didn't seem to care, casually brushing off her clothes and moving toward the door. "Thanks for the beer."

"Thanks for…the dog."

"Take care of him, Jameson."

Then she disappeared.

He stared at the closed door, wondering why the place suddenly seemed so empty.

Until a low whine interrupted his thoughts. He regarded the messy beast with an assessing gaze, and those big brown eyes stared back with a naked pleading and hope that punched him right in the chest.

Damnit. He wasn't up for this. His two lousy months had already been met with too many challenges when he'd only wanted to help out Mac and keep his head down. He had no desire to be involved with any of the locals or dog rescues but now he was stuck.

"I'll get your bed from the attic. No sleeping on the bed or the furniture. Understood?"

Bear whimpered.

Jameson sighed. "Come on. I'll show you where the food and water will be. But don't get too comfy. I'll be putting your picture up around town so you can find a real home. Deal?"

He headed toward the kitchen, stumbling when the dog bumped into his legs and almost made him face-plant. His dress pants were already full of hair, and a line of drool seemed to follow Bear wherever he went.

It may be harder than he thought to get this beast a home.

He reminded himself it wasn't his problem.

And wondered why the thought made him feel…regret.

* * * *

Two days later, Jameson was ready to lose his mind.

Things had begun so hopefully. It was the last weekend to pack in the customers before the Fur Gala, and he'd decided to push hard to dazzle the town. His contacts in New York City had come through and shipped him brand new table settings that screamed elegance and restraint. He'd gathered up the staff, galvanized them into an action plan, and completely renovated the place with all new décor.

Bright-white tablecloths replaced the dingy black. Chipped white china was switched out to square plates with silver edging and lavender napkins. The flatware was all upgraded to a heavier weight in platinum finish. The endless cheap holiday accessories were packed up and put away, from the white lights and fake Christmas trees, to the mistletoe and poinsettia centerpieces. In its place were now delicate glass bowls filled with pebbles, water, and one perfect red rose.

The old, red area rugs were gone. The new ones were more subtle, a tasteful pale gray splashed with a touch of lavender. The new colors were pleasing to the eye, and transformed the dining area into an upgraded experience.

He knew the staff disliked the changes, but Jameson believed it was for the best. They'd all been working too long in the same type of environment and that courted laziness. He was positive the new décor matched the menu and cocktail offerings. Everyone would eventually get on board and be happy.

Jameson was ready to overserve and overdeliver. Mac would be pleased.

Until Carl Perkins started off the day on a sour note.

Jameson looked up from his quick meeting with the hostess to see an overweight man lumbering through the front door dressed in a Santa suit. He was about to politely get rid of him before they officially opened, but

Layla lit up and greeted him like an old friend. "Carl! I was hoping we'd see you this weekend! How are you doing?"

Carl patted his belly and squinted through metal framed glasses that seemed to be more cosmetics than to see. His beard was a bit dingy and crooked. "Hi, Layla. Well, I've been a bit sick with my IBS, but finally feeling better. I didn't want to miss our weekend tradition but the new guy has been giving me the runaround. Left a few messages but he never got back to me. Was going to call Mac but figured I'd just show up."

Jameson tried not to groan. He'd ignored the garbled messages, which consisted of asking for a few hundred dollars in order to purchase gifts for random kids this weekend and the rental of a Santa suit. Of course, he'd deleted the messages and assumed it was a prank, or spam. This was for real?

He cleared his throat and stepped forward. "I'm the new manager, Jameson Franklin. I apologize, your messages weren't clear. What exactly were you asking to do?"

Carl gave him a once-over, then shook his head. "I play Santa the weekend before Christmas. Been doing it for Mac a couple years now. Polite thing to do is give a man a call back, right?"

He tried not to wince at being schooled on manners. "I'm very sorry, but I've been a bit overwhelmed with things around here. Trying to keep things running smoothly for Mac."

The man seemed to soften. A loud noise rumbled from his belly and Carl patted it. Jameson tried not to worry at his expression, which was pained. "Sorry, I had some milk in my coffee this morning. Not a good idea. Listen, it's not a problem. You can give me about three hundred and I'll head to the store and get the gifts. Be back here by 11am. Sound good?"

Jameson shifted his feet. "Layla, can you check with the chef that he has everything he needs? There were a few supplies that came in late."

"Sure."

He waited until she'd disappeared before turning to the man. "Thank you for the kind offer but we won't be doing Santa this year."

Carl stared. "Huh?"

"Santa. We won't be needing your services. Thank you for the offer, though."

The man scratched his head, and the wig slid partway off. He glared over the tiny spectacles. "What are you talking about? You don't cancel Santa."

He sharpened his voice to show authority. "I do. Vintage is going through some renovations so we'll be skipping the gifts and visit this year. Again, I appreciate it, but I have to get ready to open. Nice to meet you."

He turned to leave but a loud sound exploded in the air. Carl groaned and a certain smell drifted over. "Who are you—the Vintage Scrooge? The kids will be devastated. They always eat their pancakes and open presents. Why are you being so cheap? Fine, I'll do it for two hundred."

"There are no more pancakes," Jameson muttered. "And no money will be spent on useless gifts."

"What am I going to do with the suit? I already paid for it!" Another gurgling noise. "Damn dairy. I need the bathroom."

Jameson glanced at the clock. He did not need this scene to greet the first customers of a busy weekend. He needed this man out of here. "I'll cut you a check for the suit," he said, motioning him forward. "Use the office bathroom, then you can leave through the back door."

Carl bent over slightly, which loosened his beard so a bunch of gnarled gray hair hung halfway to the floor. "Fine. But this is a terrible thing you're doing. Killing kids hopes and dreams is a sin."

"I can live with that."

He wrote out a check to cash while Carl was in the bathroom destroying his private sanctuary, then hustled him out the door. By the time Vintage opened, Jameson was already a bit rattled.

The customers flooded the new space, commenting on the lack of holiday décor; the expensive bar bill; and why all the colors had changed. Jameson showed up at every table to greet the customers, explaining the exciting new updates, upselling the menu, and promising a five-star experience.

The children became a problem.

He stopped at table five, where an adorable young girl and her father were eating. Her blonde pigtails held red ribbons, and her outfit consisted of a sparkly sweater, furry pants and bright red rubber boots. Her wrist was filled with jangly bracelets and Christmas tree earrings bobbed as she tilted her head up to look at him. "Welcome to Vintage. I'm Jameson, the manager, and I'm here if you have any questions. We've been doing some updating and looking forward to any input you have for me and my staff."

"Hi, I'm Zoe! Daddy and I came to see Santa. Do you know when he'll be here?"

Her bright blue eyes fastened on him with innocent trust. He swallowed hard and tried to be a man about it. "I'm sorry but Santa won't be able to make it this weekend. He's extremely busy with his…schedule."

The father studied him with frank curiosity. He was ridiculously good-looking in a classic way, with thick dark hair, dark eyes, and a solid, confident presence. "What a shame. Hi, I'm Gabe. I work over at Sunshine Bridal. How's Mac's sister doing?"

Jameson checked in on both of his cousins regularly, but was surprised at the consistent concern of the patrons. "Much better, he appreciates so many of his friends checking on him."

"Good. I see there's been a lot of changes here. Looking forward to attending the Fur Gala."

"It will be quite a turnout. How was your meal, young lady?"

Zoe glanced at her father as if asking a question. Gabe nodded. "Mr. Jameson, I really miss the pancakes. It's my favorite part of coming here and I would like to make a suggestion, like in one your boxes? I would like to vote that you bring the pancakes and Nutella and fruit back."

He'd been dealing with complaints on the charcuterie board all morning but the way Zoe approached it made him pause. "Did you try one of our new entrees on the menu? What about the stuffed French toast?"

"Yes, that's what I got but I really really love the pancakes. Plus, it comes on a big fun board and I get to have different type of bacons. But I don't want anyone to get sad so please don't tell anyone else I was disappointed. Okay?"

He couldn't help the smile that tugged at his lips. She actually looked concerned she'd hurt his feelings. "Okay. Anything else?"

She bit her lip. "I really like the lights but they're gone. But I love the purple. Purple is my favorite color but I put red ribbons and a red sweater on because it's Christmas and red is the best."

"Thank you for the suggestion, Zoe. I will see what I can do."

Her face lit up. "Okay! Mr. Jameson?"

"Yes?"

"Since Santa is busy and lots of kids still come here to get presents, would it be okay for me to bring some over here for kids to open later on? I've been saving and Mom says it's good to give to cheerity, and I usually give to the dogs because I love dogs and have one, but this year I want to give extra presents because Santa is busy. Daddy, is that okay? We can go to the store with my piggy bank money and come back here! Plus, you don't have a tree and you need a Christmas tree to put the presents under so we can stop and get a small one!"

He blinked and glanced at Gabe.

The man gave a deep sigh. "Yeah, I know. She's hard to say no to, and I have to deal with her and Bella. Her mother's heart is just as big.

Probably the reason I fell in love with both of them on sight."

Guilt squirmed through him. Crap. Now he felt like a Scrooge instead of a good businessman. "Zoe, that's very kind. Santa would be really proud of you. But you don't have to worry because I'll take care of it here. My staff will get some presents and a tree and we'll give them out tomorrow. Okay?"

She clapped her hand. "Okay! Thank you, Mr. Jameson. You are a very nice man."

His ears felt like they were turning red. Gabe reached out to shake his hand. "A pleasure to meet you. Let me know if there's anything my wife and I can do to help with the Fur Gala. I'm sure you have your hands full."

"Thank you. Devon has been my point person on the whole thing."

Gabe's dark eyes twinkled. "Ah, Devon is the perfect person to keep it all together for you."

"Are we talking about the same woman?"

Gabe laughed. "I think so. She knows exactly how to deal with the heart of any problem without flinching and get things done. You're in good hands."

Jameson turned over those cryptic words in his head, wondering why it seemed Gabe knew her well. "Good to know. Have a wonderful rest of your day. Zoe, it's been a pleasure."

He bowed formally which made her giggle, and walked away.

The rest of the day held the same undertones. Kids cried when Santa didn't show up. Customers complained. The staff seemed miserable. The chef sent out a whipped cream sad face on the French toast, inciting giggles from the table. With each hour, Jameson became more frustrated and confused to why no one in Cape May saw his vision, and how much better Vintage was if they just gave it a chance.

He left to go home before the dinner shift and take care of Bear.

When he opened the door, he was met with a frantically happy, drooling dog with a very large piece of furniture in his mouth.

The leg of the sectional.

In growing horror, Jameson took in the damage to the house.

Pillows were torn. The sectional limped drunkenly to its side. The beach coffee table book was shredded into confetti. He'd gotten into the garbage and had a food party, so coffee grounds, banana peels, and the remains of Vintage take-out were strewn all over the kitchen floor.

"Bear. What did you do?"

The canine ducked his head for a moment, as if feeling guilty and wanting to take a moment to form an apology.

And then with a mighty leap, he jumped up, toppling Jameson over, and licked his face furiously. Jameson fought off the drool from his drippy jowls and the massive weight trying to pin him down as Bear's tail wagged with pure happiness.

Jameson was not as happy.

He was going to kill Devon.

Chapter Six

"Devon? You okay?"

She shook her head hard and re-focused on the woman across from her. Avery Sunshine, part owner of Sunshine Bridal, stared at her with a concerned look. This was the third time she'd drifted off, distracted by some odd thought of *him*.

"Sorry, I didn't sleep last night and feel a bit foggy. We decided on the red calla lilies, white roses, and lavender pine cones?"

"Yes, that's perfect. I need a coordinating flower girl bouquet, and can we bring in some mistletoe with fairy lights? I'm balancing whimsical with holiday."

"Hmm, I think mistletoe can be overdone. How about we do holly bushes and I can string the lights around like mini Christmas trees?"

"Done." Avery sat back with a sigh and smoothed back her honey-colored curls. She was a business dynamo and Devon had always admired her, along with her two sisters, Bella and Taylor, who'd created a wedding empire in the beach town. "Why does everything have to happen around the holidays? Last year, Bella got married, and now Taylor announced her and Pierce are tying the knot."

"Oh, how exciting! Are Taylor and Pierce back from Paris?"

"Yep. Her last art show exploded so she's taking a long break and came back home for a while. We're so excited."

"You'll be at the Fur Gala, right? I'd love to see everyone."

"Definitely." Her hazel eyes sparkled with mischief. "I heard about Mac's cousin. He's causing quite a ruckus at Vintage."

Surprise cut through her. "How do you know?"

Avery laughed. "Are you kidding? You've lived here for years—you should know gossip runs rampant! I heard he's changing everything over there: uniforms, menu, even décor. I heard the chef's going to quit. Plus,

Judith said if it weren't for you, the charity event would've been moved to the fire hall. No one seems to like him. Thank God I don't have any weddings scheduled there."

Devon shifted in her seat. "Well, it does take some time for him to warm up." The words tangled on her tongue as she stumbled to explain. "He comes from this fancy place in Manhattan and thinks he can help Mac make it better. I'm sure his intentions are good."

Avery snorted. "He stripped down all the holiday stuff. Can you believe it? I heard from Layla that all the fun Christmas décor was replaced with fancy table linens, and glass bowls with rocks. No white lights. No poinsettias or mistletoe. He even cancelled Santa Claus."

Devon blinked. "Carl didn't come in for the kids on the weekend?"

Avery shook her head. "Nope. Gabe and Zoe went to breakfast yesterday morning. She was devastated over the pancakes, and then found out there's no more Santa. Poor Zoe was upset and offered to break open her piggybank and buy gifts for the kids herself. Do you believe it?"

Zoe was Bella's seven-year-old daughter. Ever since Bella married Gabe, Zoe had flourished and Devon loved seeing them become a close-knit family. Which was weird, because she'd dated Gabe seriously for a while, and had even tried to get back with him after their break-up. But she was quick to realize his heart had already been taken by Bella so Devon had helped get them together. She did enjoy a good love story, even if it wasn't hers. Everyone deserved to be happy, and Gabe was special. And Zoe was one of the best humans Devon ever met. "Actually, I do. What did Jameson say to that?"

Avery gave a humph. "Said he'd take care of it, but was probably just lying to save face in front of Gabe. Carl said he almost didn't reimburse him for the Santa suit."

"Carl owns that suit, and it's pretty old," Devon reminded.

But Avery was on a tear and kept going on. "Per the grapevine, it was too expensive to give out gifts kids may not even use. In two weeks, he's turned Vintage into some French boring bistro. And you know I love a good bistro, but this seems like he's forcing a new identity on a restaurant that just isn't supposed to be highbrow. If he wants to run a fancy eating place, he should create his own. The old Merion Inn is up for sale. Or that new vacant shop next to the arcade would make a great restaurant."

"I wonder how he got all new stuff to renovate at this time of year," she murmured. It took eons for suppliers to ship out supplies.

"I'm sure he has a bunch of connections. Too bad he's ruining a good thing. After the Fur Gala I bet people will stop going to Vintage.

Poor Mac."

"Maybe he thinks he's doing all this to help Mac and it's backfiring?" she offered weakly.

Avery gave a snort. "He's doing it for himself and he's the grinch of Cape May."

Devon tried not to groan. Seemed like Jameson was going through an identity crisis, and refused to listen to the town. The idea that Avery had taken a strong dislike to him made her tummy clench. Frustration flickered. She'd hoped he'd taken the poll to heart and stopped this silly makeover, but it seemed to only propel his determination.

Why was he being so stubborn?

Avery stood up. "I better go. See you on Saturday and—" she broke off as the door opened with a clatter, and turned to see who it was.

Devon stared in shock as the topic of their conversation suddenly appeared with Bear by his side. His usual impeccable appearance was a bit marred. That slicked back hair was mussed and disheveled. His jaw held a bit of stubble. His perfectly pressed suit showed a few creases.

But it was his face that made her jaw drop. This was no longer the cool, reserved man who traded barbs like professional swordplay. No, this man's nostrils flared and his eyes smoked with frustration and testosterone temper. His fists clenched and unclenched around the leash, where Bear panted, drooling on the floor, looking at them with unrivaled joy to see new people.

"This dog is a menace and I'm giving him back," Jameson snarled.

Avery made a noise deep in her throat and stared in shock.

Devon sighed. "You lost the bet. You can't give him back until we find a home. Hi, Bear. Is he being grumpy to you?" She closed the distance between them and scratched behind Bear's ears. The canine responded by promptly falling onto his back and kicking his giant leg in ecstasy.

"That's the biggest dog I've ever seen," Avery whispered.

"Yes, we're desperate to find him a permanent home. Jameson is being kind enough to foster him until then." Devon addressed Jameson. "This is Avery Sunshine. She runs Sunshine Bridal."

He inclined his head. "A pleasure to meet you. I think I met your family member at Vintage. He was with Zoe?"

"That's my brother-in-law." Avery tilted her head and studied him with a frankly assessing gaze. "You've been making a lot of changes at Vintage."

Devon waited for his answer, patiently petting Bear.

"Yes, I am."

Silence.

Avery waited him out. He cleared his throat and finally spoke. "I'm beginning to see this town is stubborn regarding change."

Avery gave a half laugh. "Fair assessment. We also love Christmas around here, so anyone who wants to take that away, we get suspicious of."

Jameson seemed to consider her words rather than wave them off. "Understood. May I point out, that there is an underserved population of people who don't find the holiday as satisfying. I thought by giving them a place that's more neutral, they won't be drowning in sentiments of how they *should* feel. They can just be who they want and eat really good food."

Devon stared at him in surprise. It was the first real statement that gave her a hint of the man he was beneath the surface polish. Her insides warmed when she realized maybe there was a very good reason Jameson didn't like Christmas. One he wasn't about to share with a stranger.

Avery must've reached the same conclusion. "Good point." An understanding passed between them and the air dissolved of tension. Avery gave Bear a few loving pats and moved toward the door. "Thanks for helping with Bear. I'll make sure everyone knows about it. Nice to meet you."

With those cryptic words, she left.

Jameson arched a brow. "Was that code for something I missed?"

"Yep. She's going to let the town know you're not the bad guy. You were getting a terrible reputation, but Bear will give you a second chance."

His jaw firmed. "Hell, no. You need to take him back, Devon. I have too much going on to babysit an overgrown baby. He ruined Mac's house."

She winced. "What did he do?"

"What didn't he do? Chewed up the furniture, the curtains, overturned the garbage. He did everything."

"Wait—how long did you leave him alone?"

"About six hours. I came back before dinner shift to check on him. It was a nightmare."

She blew out a breath. "He can't handle being by himself for so long. Why didn't you bring him to Vintage?"

He made a low growl in his throat that was way too sexy. She wondered what type of sounds he made when he was turned on, then felt her face turn red at the thought. "I did," he grit out. "But one of the customers brought in her dog and Bear made a scene. A *big* scene. It was humiliating."

Devon stood up from the floor and brushed off her pants. "What happened?"

"It was a damn Chihuahua. A tiny little thing in a pink collar who was well behaved. The owner had her in a purse, and when she took her out, Bear spotted her. He went apeshit. Started howling and barking, rolling around in the grass as if he was being tortured. And the dog wasn't even near him! The entire restaurant came out to look and stare, and tried to offer help. I told them to ignore him and suddenly I was the bad guy being mean to my overgrown baby dog. I had to move the Chihuahua to the other room and gave them dessert on the house."

She tried hard, she really did, but a giggle escaped her lips. "A Chihuahua?"

He glowered. "Yes. I cannot deal with this anymore. You need to take him, at least during the day."

"You want to share custody?"

"No, I want you to have full custody of the beast, but I lost the bet. So, yeah, I'll take him after the dinner shift. Is that acceptable?"

She grinned, tipping her head back. "Well, the shop is small but I can put a bed by the storage so he can still see me. I guess I can live with that."

"Thank God." His muscles relaxed and he glanced around. "This is a great space. It's very...happy."

Her grin widened. "I know that's a compliment but you sound unsure."

He smiled back. "Sorry, there's nothing wrong with happy." Jameson moved around the counter to investigate the tables and shelves displaying various bouquets. The refrigerated section held double doors of clear glass where customers could gaze at individual blooms along with curated arrangements of different sizes. Multiple ones were tagged for delivery or pick up. Foiled balloons clustered in a giant bubble in the corner streaming with gaily colored ribbons. She'd set up some small Christmas trees decorated with ornaments and shimmering with tinsel. Holiday music streamed from the speakers, and filled the space with warm cheer. She enjoyed the way he poked and prodded through her displays, and made low murmurs of approval under his breath.

Devon studied him amidst the cheerful flowers. Why did he attract her so much? Was it the mystery of him, the longing to uncover secrets females couldn't resist? His male scent rose and mingled with balsam and roses. She sniffed a bit deeper, liking the mix. "What do you think?"

"I think I was wrong about you, flower girl. There's an organization beneath the happy surface. I didn't realize you managed multiple weddings here and that in the summer you do two or three per weekend."

She cocked her head. "How'd you find that out?"

"Your website. Also, the Yelp reviews are insane. You average five stars at a high rate of customers. I saw some of the pics at that Dr. Seuss type wedding—those flowers looked like they came right from the books with those puffy type heads."

She tried not to flush with pride. One of Sunshine Bridal's clients demanded a wedding based on Dr. Seuss and she'd wrangled specific rare flowers that looked like they came from *The Lorax*. "Yeah, that was one of my finer moments."

"I'm impressed." He turned to face her. Hands on hips, feet a few inches apart, his jacket stretched across his broad shoulders, cutting an intimidating figure. The black glasses perched on his nose only emphasized his sexiness. "Making good money in a small beach town isn't easy to do."

She shrugged. "Neither is running a successful restaurant in New York City. Your place averages 4.9 stars, too. The oysters and duck seem to be the most raved about."

His dark brow arched. "I see you Googled me."

"As you did to me."

The silence simmered. She felt the tension and shifted her weight. Why was she suddenly nervous? "Did Bear really have a breakdown over a ten-pound dog?"

Jameson snorted. "More like six pounds. And yes, he wailed in a very unmasculine way. Which made the Chihuahua puff out like she was hot shit, and that just pissed me off. Bear could've taken her easy."

And then she was laughing, and so was he, and suddenly he was inches away. Their gazes met and locked. The humor faded, and she found she was gripping his arm, and his palm touched her cheek, and within seconds, electricity crackled between them.

Devon was good with men. She was rarely awkward. She was confident in her body and her mind, and had no issues making the first move, or carrying through with his. But right now, a flicker of vulnerability made her pause. She stared at him, wanting something she couldn't put a name to, wondering about this complicated man before her.

"You're really pretty," he said huskily. His finger caressed her cheek, then tipped up her chin. He pressed in, slow and steady, giving her plenty of time to move away. "I've been thinking about how you drive me crazy."

"You drive me just as crazy," she retorted a bit too breathily. Her heart pounded as his mouth lowered. His breath whispered over her lips.

"I didn't expect this. I don't do messy."

A flash of temper overtook her, and then she was leaning in, grasping his jacket with her fist, challenging him with her body and words. "Then maybe you should walk away."

His hot stare was all lust and sexy demand. "Maybe I should. But I'm thinking how damn good messy can feel."

Then he kissed her.

His lips were firm and warm against hers. His movements were slow and seductive as he explored her mouth, refusing to rush. His teeth nibbled, asking for full entry, and she arched into him, wanting more. With a sigh of surrender, she let him in, and his tongue surged forward, taking the kiss to a whole other level.

He swallowed her gasp, his delicious taste of mint and coffee swamping her senses. She hung on, digging her nails into his shoulders, meeting him halfway as their tongues tangled together in a sensual battle that left her knees shaky and her body weeping with need. It was a kiss that blistered her alive, full of demand and promises, and she hung on the precipice, shocked at the depth of passion burning from within, released with every delicious thrust of his tongue. His hands burrowed in her hair, holding her head still for his ravishment. Devon hung on and gave him what he wanted, toes curling in her boots, foggy with need for more.

Oh, how she needed more.

Slowly, he retreated, still pressing tiny kisses to her swollen lips as he pulled away. Breath uneven, his eyes were like charcoal, banked fire burning into hers.

"Will you go on a date with me?"

Devon tried to find her words since she'd gone mute. She blinked and pressed her trembling fingers against her lips, still reeling from the kiss. "Huh?"

His smile was gentle. "I'm asking you out."

"Aren't we both going to the Fur Gala this weekend?"

"Technically, yes. But we're both working and I'd like to spend some one-on-one time with you."

"Okay."

"Good. How about Thursday night? I can make us a late-night supper at Vintage if you don't mind the hour."

It was an easy answer, because Devon wanted to kiss him again. "I won't mind. That works."

"Excellent."

He looked ready to leave, but her brain cells had returned and she had an important question. "What about not wanting to get messy?"

He surprised her by pressing a hard kiss to her mouth. "You convinced me it's more fun in the playground than on the sidelines watching."

Devon had no time to come up with a snappy retort.

He winked—actually winked—and was gone, the bell over the door tinkling merrily.

Dear Lord, the man had game.

She stared at Bear, sprawled out on the floor, taking up most of the precious space in the store. Then sighed. "Why do I think this whole thing could be headed toward disaster? And even more important, why am I going to do it anyway?"

Bear barked.

"Yeah, that's what I say. I guess I'll just find a cute outfit to wear and see how it goes."

Chapter Seven

He was nervous.

Jameson took a deep breath, inwardly cursing his odd surge of emotion. This was ridiculous. Asinine, really. He had no reason to freak out about seeing Devon for an actual date. He'd dated enough women in his past to feel confident and avoid first date jitters. Besides, he knew Devon—it wasn't a cold meet like on a dating app.

Yet, the kiss had disturbed him.

In a good way.

His brain once again blasted the memory of her body melting against his, the softness of her lips, the delicious taste of her. The connection had blistered hot in a way he'd never experienced before, as if he'd found his other half.

Of course, he believed in none of that nonsense, just like he believed Christmas wasn't magical. But he wanted to see her again and delve deeper. To find out more about how she came to be the woman she was.

And maybe to kiss her again.

He shook his head and finished closing up Vintage. It had been a better day, with less people complaining about the changes, yet Jameson was beginning to think he'd made some errors. He was so sure it would catch on, but the town still clung to what Vintage had been in the past. His bar bill was too low to make much of a profit. Each customer who brought in a bottle and heard there was a full bar now was stubborn enough not to want to order a cocktail. The lobster tacos were rarely ordered because everyone believed it had replaced the pancake charcuterie board. He was dealing with an element of small-town emotion he rarely encountered in the restaurant business.

Plus, he'd had to call Carl and make nice, which was a nightmare. But after his chat with Zoe, he knew he needed to at least offer a visit from

Santa. He put a placard up to advertise and brunch was completely booked. He still had a few weeks left before Mac came back, and needed to think positive. Hopefully, he'd be able to offer his cousin a more profitable, freshened up restaurant that would serve him well.

The click of heels alerted him to his date so he went to meet her at the door.

Damn, she was beautiful.

Bear bounded beside her, stretched to the maximum limit on the leash, but she never stumbled in her high platform boots. Her willowy body was clad in clingy black leggings, thigh high boots, and an emerald green sweater that made her eyes gleam like jewels. Her hair was long and loose, the pin straight strands reminding him of how satisfying it'd been to bury his fingers in them. Her lips were stained blush pink, her face bare of heavy makeup. His gaze hungrily roved over her figure, each graceful stride toward him. "Hi, flower girl. Hi, Bear."

The dog strained at the leash, so Devon unclipped him, allowing Bear to run free and almost tackle him with enthusiasm. "The beast missed you," she teased, tucking the leash into her hobo bag.

"Did anyone else?"

She laughed easily at his question, a flirty look in her eyes. "Depends on what you're feeding me, restaurant boy. I've had a busy day and I'm starving."

Jameson pet Bear, which made fur fly into the air and cling to his black pants, along with damp drool. "If you promise not to complain about the pancakes and didn't bring your own champagne, I'll dazzle you with dinner."

"Good, because I had pancakes for breakfast."

They shared an easy grin, and he led her over to a corner table he'd set up. Candles flickered in the shadows and added an intimate atmosphere. He'd already prepared the meal beforehand. "The food is ready because I know it's late. Here, take a seat."

She slid into the offered chair. "I don't mind. My schedule is a bit erratic depending on events, so I've gotten used to eating at odd times."

"Can I get you some wine?"

"Yes, please. Cabernet is perfect."

"Be right back." He went into the kitchen to finish plating and poured two glasses of wine. Bear had flopped on the floor beside the table and when he caught the scent of food, began to whine. "I got something for you, too, beast." He set the plates down, and went into the kitchen to retrieve a small bowl of cut-up filet.

Devon whistled. "Wow, we're all eating fancy tonight."

"Bear's are leftovers but don't tell him. I hate wasting good meat."

She tilted her head, lips pursed. "And ours?"

"Freshly prepared by my own hands. I hope you like it."

"It's so pretty I don't want to eat it."

Her smile made his heart stutter. He hoped to God he wasn't blushing, but watching her take the first bite was a satisfying experience. Especially after she groaned with pleasure. He'd gone with the sea bass—one of his favorite fish dishes—and paired it with a light citrus sauce over a bed of mushroom risotto. Wilted spinach with garlic rounded out the plate. Devon struck him as a woman who enjoyed simple food cooked with fresh ingredients and big flavors.

"This is insane," she said. "Sea bass is my favorite."

"Me, too. You don't eat meat, right?"

"No, I guess I'm technically a pescetarian because I eat some dairy, too."

He took a sip of his wine. Bear had gobbled up the meat in one big gulp and had rolled onto his back to nap. "Is that for dietary or something else?"

She forked up some risotto and closed her eyes halfway as she swallowed.

He got hard immediately and had to shift in his seat. God, he loved a woman who knew how to enjoy food. "No, I was a bit traumatized in my teens. I was visiting my aunt and uncle in the Catskills and they had a farm. They taught me how to do some basic things, like collect eggs and even milk the cows. For some weird reason, I bonded with one of the turkeys."

He peered over his glasses. "I'm afraid I know where this story may go."

"Yep. I didn't understand why he didn't have a name so I called him Tom."

His lip twitched. "Brilliantly original."

"Now I'm not telling you the rest."

She sipped her wine, those moss green eyes playfully challenging him. He wished he could lean over and kiss her, but she wasn't his yet. Jameson wondered what it would feel like to have that right to hold her hand, kiss her lips, stroke her hair. "I apologize. I really want to hear the rest."

"Okay, so I spent the week with Tom, having a blast. One afternoon, I went into town shopping, and when I came back, we had dinner. A turkey dinner." A sad sigh escaped her. "And I ate a lot."

A pang of sympathy hit him. "Was it good?"

She nodded reluctantly.

"When did you find out it was Tom?" he asked.

"I went looking for him the next morning. I searched for a while and then I ran to ask my uncle. Who told me quite calmly that we'd eaten him last night, and that's what turkeys were for."

He winced. "Brutal. He didn't feel the need to lie?"

Devon's fork scraped against the mostly empty plate. "He's a farmer so he never thought it was a big deal. It was just his way of life. But I didn't understand it at the time. I went hysterical and my parents decided to leave early because I was inconsolable. I vowed I'd never eat an animal again."

He liked the way she backed up her thoughts with actions. It showed the type of person she was, one of conviction. "I think that's really cool."

Devon looked up. "Thanks. I have no problem with anyone around me eating meat, it's my personal choice."

"You're okay with fish?"

She bit her lip. He wished he could have done that for her. "Kind of? I convince myself they don't experience the same pain like land animals? But I love *The Little Mermaid* and Sebastian is my favorite character. I try to avoid crab."

He laughed. "Duly noted. Did you like dinner?"

"It was perfect. Thank you, I feel so much better." She relaxed back in her chair and sipped her wine. "How'd you learn to cook so well?"

"I always loved food, but I was raised in restaurants. My mom hated to cook so very early on I knew every good place in New York. The good news was she didn't frequent fast food places. Instead, I got a great education from the local food trucks. I knew where to get the best bagels and pizza. I ate Chinese, Thai, Indian, Italian, and everything in between. Restaurants became my second home, and after my first job, I decided I needed to learn to cook."

She propped her chin in her palm and stared at him with fascination. "What a fabulous type of childhood. You found your true north so early."

"Exactly." He loved how she didn't pity him for not having a traditional mom who baked cupcakes and had a warm dinner on the table at six every night. It always bristled when people wanted to sympathize over a gift. "I've been doing it for years now and I never wanted to do anything else. It was good to start with being a bus boy and learning all the less glamorous jobs. I think you need to experience each one to be a good leader."

"Agreed. So, you're living your best life? Working at a restaurant you love. Living in a great city. Do you feel like you have it all?"

The question threw him off guard. His normal instinct was to give her a resounding yes. But inside, deep where he rarely explored, was an emptiness. He always believed it belonged to loss, from the woman he loved. A relationship that had broken his heart, so he never wanted to deal with another one. He'd kept the others to a level he could control, but Jameson was beginning to wonder if by staying safe, he'd also sacrificed the best parts. He decided to offer a safe remark. "I'm definitely happy."

Devon squinted those magnificent eyes. Her gaze delved into his, and immediately, the air between them charged. It was as if she knew about his omission, and was choosing not to ask. He had a sudden instinct being involved with Devon would demand more of him. Usually, that would urge him to walk away.

But right now, he didn't want to.

"What about your own restaurant? Do you ever think about it?"

He nodded. "I do. It's something I think about now and then, but I've been satisfied with where I am."

"Are you truly satisfied? Or complacent?"

He jerked back at the piercing question. "A big word for a big concept."

Her expression softened as she smiled. "That wasn't a jab. I was just thinking about what you told me when you wanted to change Vintage. You mentioned Mac had gotten complacent."

Oh, yeah. This woman would definitely be a challenge. "Ouch. You're right. But I think we can reach levels where it's okay to stay the course if things are good. If everyone is happy."

A wicked mischief danced over her features. "Like keeping the pancakes?"

Jameson laughed and shook his head. "That was mean."

She laughed with him. "Sorry. I mean, maybe you're right. But what if you haven't pursued the idea of your own business because it's so much easier not to? Which has nothing to do with not *wanting* to. Change is hard. It can emit failure. Regret."

He pondered her words. Was she right? How often had he looked at vacant storefronts and imagined himself creating his own restaurant? Dreamed of the menu and atmosphere and the vibe? The want had definitely been there. He just hadn't prodded the thoughts into action because—

He was complacent.

A lightbulb exploded in his head. He'd need to sit with the realization for a while and see what he wanted to do with it. Jameson leaned in, caught up in her mind and her gaze and wanting to be closer. "You may be right. What about you? Any regrets?"

She gave a delicate shrug. "Don't we all? Every path we don't take can be a regret. I try not to steep myself in that type of negativity. I tell myself I did the best I could at the time, and give myself grace. We're way too hard on ourselves, don't you think?"

Her words gave him pause. He hadn't expected that from her. She had so many different layers hiding under the surface beauty. "I think that concept is extremely underrated and under used. I think if we did that more often, we'd take a hell of a lot more risks."

Silence fell. It was full of want, of possibilities, of a gentle peace and simmering excitement he'd never experienced. At this very moment, he felt poised on the precipice of something special.

Her voice rose to his ears in a lilting caress. "I didn't expect this."

"Me either."

"I didn't really like you."

"Me either."

Her lower lip twitched in humor. She lifted her glass and drank the last ruby red drops of wine. "It's getting late. I really need to go."

"Coffee? Dessert?"

Devon shook her head. "I have a lot to do tomorrow for the Fur Gala. I'd like to decorate early Saturday morning before customers come in."

"That's not a problem. I'll be here to help you."

Her brow arched. "Thought you weren't going to offer any assistance, remember?"

He winced. "I do. Let's say things have…changed."

Neither of them said what they were thinking. Jameson let her have the space. Things had turned fast between them, and she needed to get her footing. Even he felt a bit topsy turvy with how close he suddenly felt to her in such a short time, and it had all started out not liking each other.

Yeah. Things had definitely changed.

"I'll walk you to the car."

Devon hooked Bear to the leash and stood. Jameson offered his hand. Her fingers entwined with his as they threaded their way to the back door and down the stone path. The graveled parking lot was empty. Darkness enshrouded them by the empty tennis courts. The Physick Estate behind the restaurant glowed with holiday lights. The winter air was cold and sharp and still. Thick clouds blocked the moon.

Bear trudged beside. "When do you want to drop him off tomorrow?" she asked.

"Eight am, okay?"

"Yes." She turned to face him, her back to the car. "Thank you for dinner. It was amazing."

"Thank you for joining me. I enjoyed cooking for you."

Underneath his polite words, Jameson's entire body throbbed with need. Her cheeks were flushed with cold. Her hair surrounded her like a silk curtain, and those big green eyes stared up at him, filled with a mysterious myriad of emotion he craved to figure out. The scent of florals and pine drifted to his nostrils.

"See you tomorrow," she said.

"Yes, see you tomorrow."

She twisted to open the car door. His feet were frozen to the ground, his fingers clenched into tight fists. His heart beat savagely in his chest and he tamped down hard on his animal need to touch her.

The door opened.

They moved at the same time.

Jameson stepped forward and she kicked the door closed, turning right into his arms. He gave a low growl of satisfaction as her warm, soft body crashed against his, and he cupped her chilled cheeks, stamping his mouth over hers.

Politeness and hesitation fell away. Tonight, the kiss was raw and passionate and bold. She opened beneath him and demanded more, wrapping her arms around his neck tight, hanging on. His hands drifted to cup her rear, squeezing the full globes and lifting her to meet his hungry mouth. The kiss was deep and long and dirty, and Jameson reveled in every single second.

He backed her up against the car. She gave a sexy little moan and he captured it, his tongue tangling with hers, his hands urging her legs to open so he could step between them and feel more of her. Sparks caught fire. He was hard and aching, and his head spun with a need that clawed from his gut to claim her. To give her pleasure. To fuck her so well and so long, all she could do was cry his name.

The primitive roar of instinct to imprint himself on this woman he held took him off guard.

He ripped his mouth away from hers, his breath ragged as he stared at her in the trickling moonlight.

Lips swollen and damp, she blinked up at him, obviously as foggy as him. Her pupils were dilated black with desire. Jameson ruthlessly tamped down the wild need inside, his grip gentling as he tried to regain his sanity. This was too much. Too much...

Messiness.

But God, he wanted it. Wanted Devon Pratt.

His fingers practically shook as he carefully tucked some flyaway strands behind her ear. Slowly, she began to rouse from the buzz. "Well, that's twice you managed to surprise me."

He kept his words light though his insides were raw. "Ditto, flower girl. But you deserve a hell of a lot more than being laid out on the hood of the car."

A sexy smile tugged her lips. She leaned forward and pressed a kiss to his mouth. "Not a bad idea for another time. Good night, Jameson."

This time, she opened the door, slid into the driver's seat, and took off.

He stared at the taillights with a stunned expression that felt frozen to his face.

That woman had game.

Oh, he was toast. He was already half in love with her and it made no sense.

Even worse?

He didn't want to make sense of any of it. Wanted to follow this through to the bitter end and if the whole thing blew up, Jameson had a feeling Devon Pratt would still make the end worth the ride.

Bear pushed at his chest, reminding him it was cold and he wanted to get home. "Sorry, beast. You're with me tonight, even though I'd rather have her."

Bear grinned, sloppy with drool.

Jameson laughed and led his dog home.

Chapter Eight

She walked into Vintage and took a moment to admire her handiwork.

It was beautiful. Jameson had allowed her to go hog wild with Christmas decorations and hadn't even complained. Sure, she'd caught a few grunts at the classic mistletoe, and he looked at the endless colored and white lights like they were his enemy. But this past week he'd changed. Softened.

Maybe it was the kissing.

The outside patio was outfitted with large heaters amidst the tables adorned with red cloths, high white candlesticks, beautiful pine centerpieces, and photos of the dogs. Wreaths and mini Christmas trees lined the edges brimming with colored glass balls and topped with stars. "Frosty the Snowman" belted from the speakers amidst barks, panting, and the occasional worried whimper.

Her gaze traveled over the gorgeously dressed guests all paired with dogs. Each person or couple had adopted a dog for the evening, and was able to spend some one-on-one time with the lucky canine in a roped off area dubbed the Meet n Greet. Jameson's staff brought around finger foods and mimosas on holiday platters. The double doors were open to the interior tent where a buffet would be served and dancing offered by one of the local singers.

Her favorite part was the Doggy Bar. It was filled with bones, treats, and toys for each of the dogs to indulge in. The auction table was nicely padded with gift certificates, baskets, and fun goodies to bid on.

There were six dogs as the main guests. Each were adorned with red and green collars with little bells. They'd been groomed and pampered and carefully chosen as mascots because they were good with people and crowds. If they were able to get homes, it would free up precious shelter and foster space, allowing Judith to take in more rescues who needed help.

Her heart gave a twinge at the knowledge Bear couldn't be here to strut his stuff. His fear of other dogs made it impossible to bring him, so she'd taken some photos and turned them into mini displays to showcase his goofy grin and sweet personality. She'd agreed with Jameson leaving him home for a few hours would be more bearable than being with his own peers.

Everything looked perfect. She'd been racing around nonstop doing finishing touches until Jameson ordered her to go home and get ready. Judith was finally out of quarantine and had managed to take over the rest of the activities, so Devon had felt okay coming a bit late.

She took a deep breath and headed in, but she was immediately halted by a line of people wanting to chat. She managed to grab a mimosa and then turned on the charm, schmoozing with the locals and business owners to talk up the rescue and all they did amidst gossip about the town, politics, the housing rental shortage, the beach cleanup, and a variety of other topics.

Devon relaxed into her role, enjoying the social chatter. She bent down and balanced on high heels while petting and speaking with the dogs. Beethoven was a friendly Australian cattle dog with brown and white spots who drew a lot of interest. Two poodle mixes in inky black happily chewed and played with their togs from the dog bar. Devon spotted Virginia Woof, the German Shepherd in the far corner, cocking her head with interest as she surveyed the crowd. The goofy terrier tore around outside, a bit too enthusiastic to be dignified. And of course, Willow the Queen Bee of Chihuahuas was being carried around like the royal she was.

Devon knew she'd go fast to some lucky owner.

Judith and Vishya drifted over and greeted her with hugs and excitement. The owner of the rescue looked elegant with her white hair cut into a short bob and a winter cream wool dress. Her blue eyes were kind yet sharp, and Devon had learned she was both a softie and ruthless when it came to her business of helping dogs. "Devon, you've literally saved us this season," Judith said. "The place looks like a winter festival, it's absolutely perfect. I just wasn't up to dealing with the gala—the brain fog has been terrible."

She shook her head in sympathy. "Covid is rough and hits us all different. I'm just happy you're better and thriving again. And don't thank me—Vishya has been amazing at the rescue. He entrusted Bear to me instead of sending him to another shelter."

Vishya gave her a high-five. He wore a fancy green suit with a red

Hawaiian shirt opened at the neck. Somehow, he pulled it off beautifully.

"Speaking of Bear, how is he? I heard Jameson has been helping out with taking care of him?" Judith asked.

Devon caught the judgy look in her gaze but couldn't blame her. Jameson's reputation had taken a hit in the town, especially when he tried to get out of hosting the gala. "Yes, and he's been wonderful," she said smoothly. "They've formed a bond, which is important. We just need to get Bear some help with accommodating other dogs. It's a big restriction for an adoptee to take on."

Vishya and Judith shared a look. "We may have some issues getting a behaviorist in," Judith said.

"I'm sure we'll make it work," Vishya cut in, always the lovable peacemaker. "Let's focus on the animals here tonight and getting them placed. Or at least, getting us lotsa money."

Devon relaxed and pushed further into the crowd to grab one of Jameson's mini lobster rolls. She was about to take a mouthwatering bite when the back of her neck prickled with awareness. Slowly, she cranked her head around.

Then sucked in her breath.

He was gorgeous.

The tuxedo was classic, simple black, and obviously custom made to fit his form. His thick hair was neatly slicked back, exposing his highbrow, carved cheekbones, and clean shaven, square jaw. His eyes glittered and smoked behind his glasses, which only added to his appeal. Her fingers curled into fists as she imagined touching him again, smoothing the jacket over his shoulders, caressing the lean muscled length of his arms.

He walked toward her.

Devon felt as if the room and all the people surrounding her faded away. It was like one of those movies she'd watch and make fun of, not imagining any man holding that type of rapt attention in the middle of a noisy, glittering crowd.

But Jameson Franklin owned her with each step closer. He eased past tight clusters of groups with his gaze fastened only on her.

"You look beautiful."

The compliment was simple, but it was the hunger and want in his stare that made the words come alive. Her voice was husky when she managed to speak. "So do you."

A smile touched his lips. "Are you happy with the way things turned out?"

"Yes, everything's perfect." Devon couldn't stop herself from reaching out and touching his red tie. "You dressed up for Christmas."

His smile deepened. "I dressed up for you, Devon."

The breath whooshed out of her lungs. The sexual tension swirled around them like a cloud. It took her a few moments to realize people glanced at them curiously, as if they noticed the connection. Thank goodness she was used to it and didn't care.

But poor Jameson may find himself the main topic of gossip tomorrow that had nothing to do with the dogs.

Still, she didn't move away. "Last week, you warned me the food would be simple so you didn't waste money."

"That's right."

"I see lobster rolls, scallops wrapped with bacon, mini sliders, and crab cakes. Those aren't cheap."

His shoulders moved in a shrug. "I had leftovers."

"You're making specialty cocktails, too. I was informed there would only be budget wine and light beer."

"We used the cheap vodka and no-name rum. Your dress makes me think of bad things."

She jerked. Her heart pounded wildly and her body peaked at his words, ready to play. Devon had taken particular care with her outfit for this exact reason. The silky, gold fabric wrapped around her like a present, clinging to all her curves. The V-neckline was generous. She'd twisted her hair up in an elegant braid that showed off her naked skin. "Bad in a bad way? Or bad in a good way?"

A low growl escaped his throat. "Oh, very good. Uncomfortably good."

"That is a slim cut designer suit you're wearing. Must be difficult."

He threw back his head and laughed. More glances cut their way. She grinned, cheeks flushed, and wished desperately they were alone. Suddenly, Jameson reached out and snagged her around the waist, a public declaration so bold and so sexy, shivers raced down her spin. "Devon—"

Jordan interrupted with her usual drama, sporting a black mini dress that showed off her perfect legs. "There you are! I was stuck outside while Dooby played ball. Sistine got trapped by Caesar, who won't shut up about the influx of city people buying all the properties and renting out to tourists, so she needs rescuing ASAP. Oh, hi, Jameson."

He dropped his hand from her waist and pushed his glasses back up the bridge of his nose. "Nice to see you again, Jordan."

Jordan grunted, obviously not sharing the sentiment.

Devon bit her lip as her bestie treated him to a cold look. The last time they'd spoken, Jameson had been enemy number one. With all the chaos this week, and her friend buried in wedding dress madness, they hadn't spoken. She'd have some explaining to do once Devon admitted she'd had a complete change of heart and was now seriously thinking of dragging the enemy into her bed.

Devon grabbed her friend's hand. "Let's go get Sistine," she said brightly, shooting Jameson an apologetic look. "I love your dress."

"Thanks. You look gorgeous as usual." Jordan tossed her hair in dismissal and followed her across the room. "I'm sorry I couldn't save you sooner from the asshole. Ugh, it was like he stuck like glue to your side. Gross."

She winced. "So, about that. I forgot to tell you that things have changed. He's not a bad guy after all."

Jordan rolled her dark eyes. "Riiight. He just ruined Vintage, tried to cancel the Fur Gala, fired Santa, and tried to get you to do all the work for this event last minute. He's a Georgia peach."

"No, Jordan, I mean it. He's not what we thought. He's...kind of nice."

"You've had too much to drink. You didn't smoke before this, did you?"

A frustrated laugh escaped her lips. "No!"

"I can't believe I called him hot! He's really not that good looking, either. Way too stiff and reserved to translate to anything good. Can you imagine how robotic he'd be in bed?"

She was going to D.I.E.

Sistine interrupted with a shriek, hugging her tight, and obviously not trapped by Caesar. Clad in a scarlet jumpsuit, her red hair a tumble of waves down her back, Sistine was a stunner and the sweetest human on the planet. "You haven't checked in all week," Sistine complained. "Jordan was working extra shifts at Vera's Bridal and you were imprisoned by the Grinch of Cape May. I was lonely."

"I missed you, too. But I have to tell you both something. It's about Jameson. I—"

Sistine jumped in. "Jordan told me everything. He's horrible. He took away the pancakes! He made you do all the work when poor Judith was sick. I mean, sure, Avery said he took Bear to help you out but I think it was in his master plan to pretend to be nice so he could get customers back to eat here. People have decided to ban Vintage until Mac gets back."

Devon rubbed her temple. When her friends got revved up, it was almost impossible to get in a word. She raised her voice to be heard over the music and the chatter and the dogs. "Please listen for a moment! I didn't get to tell you because it happened so fast but I changed my mind about Jameson."

Jordan waved her hand in the air. "You are way too nice, Devon. Always the first to forgive, or give second chances, but babe, don't waste your time on this guy. He's a cheap carbon copy of his cousin and an outsider. Soon, he'll go back to New York and things will return to normal."

"Agreed," Sistine said. "We love you, Devon. Don't even think about him."

"Dammit, I need to say something now!"

Jordan patted her hand, which made her grit her teeth in frustration. "Sure. We'll talk later."

There was a high pitch behind her, like a speaker was cranking. A loud voice cut through the room with some type of announcement, turning Sistine and Jordan's head, and Devon lost her temper, needing to let them know the truth.

Gathering her breath, she raised her voice as loud as she could.

"I like Jameson Franklin! I think he's hot!"

The words exploded into a suddenly silent room.

Frozen in shock, she half closed her eyes. *No. No, no, no...*

It seemed like centuries before she gathered the courage to turn slowly around. Jordan and Sistine gaped at her. Jameson stood at the front of the room, a microphone in his hand, surrounded by dozens of locals who began to titter and smile and murmur to each other while they all stared.

Devon fell mute as the horrific nightmare of this faux de pau struck her full force.

She had humiliated both of them at the holiday Fur Gala.

Miserable, red with embarrassment, Devon waited for him to say something.

Jameson cleared his throat. "As I was saying, the buffet is now open. Please proceed into the back and help yourself."

Oh, hell. She was getting out of here.

Pivoting on her high heels, she took a desperate step toward the door.

His voice rumbled over the speakers. "Oh, one last thing. I happen to be crazy about Devon Pratt. And I think she's sexy as hell."

Mic drop.

Chapter Nine

Well, that had been unexpected.

Jameson fell into his host role as the evening wrapped up. His staff were already hard at work in the kitchen and had dismantled the buffet as the crowd moved out to the patio to sip after dinner drinks and complete the silent auction. He thanked the guests as they dispersed, and kept his face impassive, yet polite, as every single one of them asked about his new relationship with Devon.

He gave the same response each time. "We're getting to know one another right now."

No more and no less.

Even though, inside, all he wanted was to get rid of everyone so he could kiss her senseless.

"It was a wonderful event," a deep voice said behind him. He turned and shook Gabe's hand, who was with his lovely wife, Bella. Bella looked exactly like Zoe in adult form. Jameson immediately felt comfortable around the Sunshine sisters and their spouses. Each of the women emanated a warm energy and unique personality he appreciated.

Avery, as the oldest, seemed to be the leader. He'd caught her ordering her sisters around while Bella sweetly agreed and Taylor sarcastically challenged. Taylor, as the youngest, sported pink hair and a no-bullshit demeanor. Her husband, Pierce, acted relaxed and laid back. When Jameson had engaged them in conversation, they'd finished each other's sentences and struck him as true soul-mates.

The same could be said for Avery's husband, Carter, who'd carried their Yorkshire terrier, Lucy, around in a bold pink tote without apology.

"Thanks for coming tonight. Tell Zoe I said hello."

Taylor leaned against Pierce and stared at him with curiosity. "I like the changes you made at Vintage," she said. "Then again, I was never a big fan of the pancakes here."

He laughed. "Appreciate it. We'll see what happens. By the way, I heard the painting in Mac's house was created by you. It's seriously the only thing I love there. You've got serious talent."

She brightened. "Thanks. That series was one of my favorites to paint."

"Inspired by me," Pierce added, earning a playful punch on his arm.

"How's Bear doing? Why wasn't he here tonight?" Avery asked.

"He doesn't do well with other dogs. We'll need to get him some training, so he's home, destroying Mac's house."

Carter chuckled. "Sounds about right. Lucy refused to even look at Avery when we first met. They're possessive of their owners."

"But now she loves me more. Right, baby?" Avery cooed at the tiny princess like dog.

"Our puppy was a terror when we first got him," Gabe added. "Bella was a bit put off that I'd let Zoe have her way."

"But now I love him more," Bella teased. "Dogs seem to do that. It's hard to fight when all they want is to give and receive love with no other expectations."

"True," Jameson said. "I never had much exposure to animals. My place is tiny in New York, and my shifts are insane. Nothing lives for too long. I managed to kill a cactus."

The sisters all shared a knowing glance. "Things change," Bella practically sang. "Cape May is a great place to open up a restaurant."

"Lots of open spaces to get creative," Avery added.

Taylor groaned. "Cut it out, guys. Leave him alone and let's get the hell out of here. He wants to be alone with Devon."

Jameson refused to be embarrassed like a teenager but felt his ears turn red.

They all exited in a rush of chatter and barbs and he realized if he was in Cape May, they'd all probably become friends.

Not that he lived in Cape May. Or ever would. He was a city guy at heart.

Pushing away the thought, he kept busy and soon, the last of the guests had gone. His staff finished dismantling and cleaning, and finally, he was left alone in Vintage.

With Devon.

Her heels clicked on the floor as she walked over. "All set?" she asked lightly.

"Yep. Hell of an evening, huh?"

He noticed she avoided his probing gaze, turning slightly away. "Yes, it was. Heading home to Bear now?"

"Yep. Thing is, I'm terrified of what I'll find when I get there. He may be frantic, and I don't think I can handle it alone right now."

That made her chin tilt up. "Do you need help?"

He kept his face neutral. "It would mean a lot to me. I think Bear could use the extra company. Can you come with me to Mac's house?"

She shifted her feet. Paused. "Well, if you think I could help."

"I do. Did you have a lot of champagne?"

She picked up the suggestion and gracefully volleyed. "I had a few glasses. Maybe it's better if I left my car here and you drove?"

"Smart idea."

They walked out to the car side by side. He brushed his fingers against hers.

The drive was short and completed in silence, but it wasn't tension that stopped them from speaking. Jameson felt the sweet tight anticipation between them like a beautiful dance. Neither wanted to ruin it with words.

Bear greeted them with the mad fury of a canine scorned but after a potty trip, a snack, and some extra affection, the beast finally settled. Jameson took two cans of seltzer out of the refrigerator, poured them into glasses, and handed her one. She took it with a nod and prowled around the rooms, studying the various books on the shelves.

He tamped down a grin, allowing her the space, allowing her to feel comfortable about what was about to happen. And it would happen.

On her terms.

"The auction went well. We brought in a lot of money for the shelter. Judith cried."

He nodded, sipping his seltzer. "You had some great items to sell."

"Yeah, except that ridiculous portrait prize. It started at three hundred dollars. I doubted it'd sell to anyone. Who wants a caricature of yourself done over Zoom? Marilyn has a wonderful heart, but she does those drawings on the side and no one has the heart to tell her they're awful."

Jameson kept his expression mildly interested. "I hope she wasn't hurt by not selling it."

Devon tapped her lip thoughtfully. "That's the thing that puzzled me. Someone did bid on it. At three hundred dollars. It'd be the most she'd ever made in her life."

"Wow, I guess someone was trying to be nice. Good for her."

Slowly, she put her glass on the table. He did the same.

"It was you. You bought that awful caricature for a stupid price and you used the name Frank James. Clever."

He blinked. "Not very clever if you figured it out."

She blew out a breath and faced him head on. Feminine energy sparked around her and turned her eyes to emerald fire. She clenched her fists and breathed deep, and the satiny fabric of her dress clung to her breasts like a gift from God, for his eyes only. His body tightened with a ravenous hunger, but he kept still, allowing her to set the pace. "Why are you doing this?"

His tone was mild but his body was at war, practically shaking under his clothes. "Doing what?"

"This!" Her hand cut through the air and she trembled. His gaze carefully took in her hard nipples and flushed skin, knowing he was so close. "You make this ridiculous donation to a cause you never even believed in, and you upgraded the appetizers and drinks and even added halibut to the buffet! You can't make a profit on halibut at a charity buffet."

"Yep, I took a bath on that one."

"Stop, just stop. Then you say these…things about me over the microphone? When you know how this town gossips? Everyone will be bugging you about how you feel about me, and give you all this pressure, and you're going to regret it. Big time."

"Doubt it."

She lost it. With a screech of rage, she stomped over to him and faced him toe to toe. "Why did you lie to me? Why are you so different from what I thought!"

Head thrown back, breath puffing through her pink lips, hair disheveled and coming out of her fancy braid, she was everything he'd ever dreamed of or wanted in a woman and he couldn't wait another second.

Jameson moved, grabbing her around the hips, lifting her up so they were nose to nose, mouth to mouth, inches away. "Because somehow, some way, you make me want to do better."

Her eyes widened in shock. "Damn you for ruining everything." Then she grabbed his shoulders, jerking him forward, and kissed him.

They exploded together like a tsunami hits the shore. Wrapping her legs tight around his hips, their mouths fused hungrily, desperate for each other, and Jameson wanted to drown in her taste and smell and feel until there was nothing left of him but her.

He walked her into the bedroom, palms roving over her back, never breaking the kiss. The fabric of her dress crushed around him, hiked up to her hips. Placing her on the bed, they shed their clothes in a frenzy, throwing each item on the floor, stopping to kiss and stroke every bare expanse of flesh as it was revealed.

He tugged down her dress straps and groaned as her breasts spilled into his hands. He stroked and cupped the heavy weight, loving the cherry red of her nipples, sucking tight on the hard nubs as he relished her cries. She pulled at buttons and the belt buckle, practically ripping off the fancy vest. Her fingers played in the swirls of hair on his bare chest, drifted downward, and then she shoved both hands in his boxers to cup his erection.

He hissed out a curse. Holy crap, he wouldn't last long at this rate. This woman was pure fire. "Sweetheart, you gotta slow down."

"Can't. Keep up, restaurant boy."

His half laugh, half groan was swallowed by her mouth over his, so he kicked his pants free of his ankles and toppled her down on the bed.

Slipping the dress free, he tugged the slinky fabric down her hips and stared at her gorgeous, mostly naked body. A tiny pair of black lace panties barely covered her. He'd fantasized of taking her panties off with his teeth, and teasing her until she was helpless and begging.

Unfortunately, he had no time for that.

He took the sexy underwear off and gazed at her perfect, bare mound. Pushed her thighs slowly apart. Tossed his glasses onto the floor. Dipped his head.

And licked.

She cried out, her hands buried in his hair as he pleasured her with his teeth and tongue and lips, drunk on her taste. He nipped at her swollen clit, laving it with his tongue, and her voice got hoarser as she arched up hard in feminine demand.

He gave her everything she wanted and more until she fell apart under his tongue, his name a ringing scream in his ear.

Jameson didn't stop licking her until the last of convulsions had passed. He rolled half to the side, shoving open the night stand drawer, grabbed a condom and sheathed himself.

Propped up between her wantonly spread legs, he gazed at her with a raw hunger that made him feel uncivilized. Cheeks flushed, lips parted, hair falling across her naked breasts, she was a vision. He could spend hours just looking at her, exploring every dip and curve of her body, but right now, he needed to be inside her more than his next breath.

Devon slid down, hooking her legs around his hips, guiding him toward her damp heat. He took her lips in a rough kiss, and when he broke away there was a lust in her eyes that took away the last of his control.

She whispered the words in his ear. "Fuck me, Jameson."

With a hiss, he pushed inside, slow and steady, sinking deep.

His entire body shuddered with pleasure. Muscles locked, he began to move, slow at first, then faster as she grabbed his shoulders, nails biting into his skin, urging him on. He took her on a wild ride and she met him at every thrust, every cry, every stroke. Watching her face, she fell apart piece by piece, biting her lip as the orgasm took her. He slammed his hips forward one final time and let himself go.

He didn't remember much after. It was as if the sex was too intense to make sense of what had happened between them. Jameson disposed of the condom and brought her water. Bear trotted into the room now that it was safe, and lay by the bed, happily snoring away a few moments later. Devon was sprawled out in the sheets, one long leg falling partway off the mattress, face smashed into the pillow. He climbed in beside her, caressing her perfect ass, smoothing up her back and pushing her hair aside.

Pressing a kiss to the nape of her neck, he pulled her into his body.

And slept.

Chapter Ten

That night changed everything.

Jameson was used to talking things out with his lovers and structuring rules. Defining expectations. Not because he was unromantic, but he found things worked smoother when all parties communicated. He liked to be clear about his limitations so he didn't hurt anyone.

With Devon, they woke up in the morning and they were together.

He'd reached for her multiple times in the darkness, insatiable for more. A fierce connection thrummed between them on a scale he'd never experienced. There was no thought to anything but the knowledge he needed to be with her.

Jameson waited for her to ask about their relationship, or question what they were doing. After all, he only had a few weeks left here before Mac returned and then he'd go back to his real life.

Except Devon was slowly becoming his real life.

And she never asked. They fell into a routine over the next week naturally. They ate breakfast together, went to their jobs, and touched base during the day. Devon came to Vintage with Bear every evening after she closed the shop. They'd hang together for the final hour before close, then head back to either Mac's house or her apartment for the evening. They'd stay up late talking and making love, until they fell into an exhausted sleep for a few hours.

She'd been right about the gossip. He couldn't go anywhere without curious looks and low murmurs. Every table at Vintage poked and prodded him with questions about Devon. He smiled politely and repeated the same staged line over and over. Devon said they were doing the same in her flower shop and business had never been better.

He made some final changes at Vintage, serving dinner late for Christmas Eve and closing Christmas day. When she asked if there was any place he needed to be for the holidays, he told her no.

She'd just smiled and responded with the same.

They spent Christmas and New Year's together, staying late at Vintage with Bear, nursing a glass of champagne under the mistletoe he never took down.

It was the best holiday he'd ever had.

Jameson knew time was running out for both of them. Eventually, a decision needed to be made.

He just didn't know if he could make it.

* * * *

Devon collapsed on her sofa, groaning at the ache in her feet. Of course, things had been going so well, she was due for a wedding from hell. For some strange reason, January brides were the worst. Maybe they were cranky they missed the holidays, or that the beach town was suddenly stripped of lights and gaiety as everyone shut down until spring. She still didn't have a valid reason except the next few weeks would be torturous since nothing made them happy.

Avery and Bella had done everything in their power to create perfection at the Sea Salt, but everything had been cursed. The bride's father-in-law spilled a tumbler of tequila on her dress and she stank like a distillery. A fight broke out with two of her cousins and ended in a fist fight on the dance floor. For Devon's part, she'd been delivered fifteen dead bouquets from her custom supplier and had gone into overdrive trying to pull together replacements. Of course, the bride noticed the switch-out and burst into tears. Devon had to heavily discount the fee and deal with a bad review.

She just wanted to see Jameson.

Even his name brought a silly smile to her lips and a lurch in her tummy. Devon wasn't the type of woman who cared about a certain time before she had sex—it was all gut instinct and what felt right. She wasn't big into declaring rules up front either, and sensed Jameson worked the same way.

Except...

She'd never fallen into a heavy relationship after two weeks and one night together.

Jordan and Sistine insisted they all hang out the day after Christmas before they could officially approve him. When she mentioned it, Jameson agreed, and they'd shared a drink after supper. After a tense beginning, they soon fell into easy chatter and her friends had declared him good enough for her to sleep with.

For Devon, it was the last hurdle.

A tap at the door brought Bear barreling forward, whining with fervor. She limped over and opened it.

Jameson picked her up and kissed her. She immediately melted into him; body familiar with every hard muscle. She stroked his glossy hair and savored the rough stubble on his cheeks. Her nostrils hummed with every delicious breath of his musk scented skin. She always knew she was a passionate person and sex was an important factor for her in a relationship. But never in her life had she imagined the sensuality and intensity of Jameson Franklin. He practically seethed with virility once unleashed and she loved every moment.

His teeth nipped at her bottom lip, then sucked. Her head spun.

Bear barked.

"Sorry, beast, you're next." Shooting her a grin, he released her and gave Bear his demanded attention. There was a bond between them now, evident in the way Jameson thought about not only the dog's needs but his wants. That gentle, beautiful heart of his burned bright and strong, and Devon was lucky to have discovered it.

"I can't imagine I once thought of you as the Grinch," she commented.

"I think it was Scrooge. I was being tight with my pennies, remember?"

"Yeah, that's right. How come you're here? I thought I was meeting you after work."

"Because you had the wedding from hell and I figured I'd leave a bit early to come to you."

"Are you like this with all your girlfriends?" she asked teasingly.

She waited for him to tease back, but his features tightened. "No, I wasn't," he said. A raw truth edged his words, and she tilted her head, waiting. "I think I was a pretty lousy lover in the past."

"Physically I think that's impossible."

His lip twitched. "Emotionally. Mentally. Respectfully." He seemed to get lost in thought. "I held myself back because I was too worried about my needs. My career. My place. My friends. My money. My relationships never lasted long, and I always believed I was this guy who was above reproach, wanting to be honest about my limitations."

She felt close to a big reveal, something that would allow a deeper piece of himself to unlock and share with her. "And now?"

His gaze locked with hers. "Now I think I was full of bullshit. I just didn't want to take the chance."

Something shifted between them. Devon wanted to ask more questions, but sensed it wasn't the time to push. "I'm not perfect either. I've made mistakes."

"Earth-shattering mistakes? Or more like taking away pancakes from everyone who loved them?"

She laughed and pushed her hair back. "Like being happy with surface relationships because they looked good. Fit my expectations of the type of man I should be with."

He lifted a brow. "Like Gabe?"

Her mouth fell open. "How do you know about that?"

"Oh, trust me, I heard it all from good-natured, well-meaning gossipy locals."

"What else did you hear?" she asked suspiciously.

He ticked them off his fingers. "You dated Gabe hot and heavy for a while, then broke up. Then you roomed with a woman named Lily for six months which was supposedly your transitional. Then you broke up and tried to get back with Gabe, but he was in love with Bella so you let him go."

"I cannot believe this," she muttered, shaking her head. "I hate small towns."

"It was fascinating. Want to expand on any of it?"

Devon rolled her eyes and marched toward the kitchen to grab two seltzers. "No. Except Lily and I were never involved in that type of relationship. She's a childhood friend who was going through some stuff and moved in with me for a while. Someone saw us hugging and me kissing her on the lips—a friendly peck in greeting—and that was it for the rumor mill."

"Did it bother you?"

"No, I didn't really care. No one was judging me. At least, no one I deal with on a personal basis."

She turned, ready to hand him the seltzer, but the look in his eyes made her pause. Immediately, she grew damp between her thighs. He stalked across the room and stood before her. She shivered.

"The more time I spend with you, the more I want you."

Slowly, he took the can and touched it to her lips. The iciness burned, but he rolled it softly, barely brushing her mouth. Moving it downward, he touched her nipples, coasted down her stomach and kicked her legs apart.

Then pressed the can between her legs.

She cried out, and he yanked her against him, kissing her wildly. They sunk down to the floor and as she tumbled on top of his hard body, Devon wondered how she'd ever be able to watch him leave.

* * * *

After taking out Bear and settling him in, they made it to bed.

"Tell me, flower girl. How did I get lucky enough to find you single?" He pressed kisses to her stomach, her breasts, worshiping each inch of skin with his lips and tongue and teeth. He savored her tiny moans and the way she arched into his touch. She made him ravenous for more, to devour her whole, even though he'd claimed her twice already.

"I could say the same for you." Suddenly, her head shot up and her gaze narrowed. "Wait—you are single, right?"

"Yes. I'm not a cheater." He bit gently into her inner thigh for punishment. She curled her toes and stretched into the pain. Hmm, he'd need to explore that more. Devon kept surprising him in and out of bed. He had a feeling he could spend a lifetime being surprised.

"Sorry, just checking. I've been happy single and I've been happy in relationships. It's not like I'm desperate to get married or have kids." She paused, but he stayed silent, wanting her to share more. "I've always felt that no matter how my life turned, I would be okay with it. But lately, I've been thinking about more. It's not about society establishments, or watching my friends all settle down, either. I just want to share my life with someone. Someone to be with me through the ups and downs, the travel, the laughs, the tears. To watch Netflix with, or tell my bad dreams to. I'm not looking for someone to fill me up. I've filled myself up."

"You want someone to stand beside you," he said, staring up her gorgeous naked body to look her in the eyes.

Relief flickered over her delicate features. "Exactly."

"You deserve that, Devon. I think we all do, especially when you build a beautiful life. Why wouldn't you want to share it?"

He loved the way she expressed herself. Jameson found himself looking at things differently when he was around her. He liked who he was better, too.

Her fingers coasted over the simple black rose tattooed on his wrist. The startled expression on her face when they made love the second time haunted him. She'd studied his ink with an intense curiosity, her gaze hesitant as she realized it was a rose, and probably for another woman. There were no initials or name. Just a simple, elegant scrawl so he'd always remember.

Finally, she'd asked one simple question. Was it for another woman?

He'd given the only answer possible.

Yes.

Nodding, she'd dropped the subject and never brought it up again. But her fingers burned as she outlined the petals and stalk, along with the one tiny thorn adorning the stem. Jameson was beginning to wonder if the memory he'd inked into his skin had been a foretelling. A change from bittersweet grief to the most dangerous emotion of all.

Hope.

"Jameson?"

He held his breath and wondered what she'd ask. If he'd tell her everything. "Yes?"

"Is a rose your favorite flower? Or your worst?"

God, he was crazy about her. Loved how she probed on her own terms, yet allowed him plenty of time to breathe in between the intensity. He felt as if his soul's outer layers were being peeled back one by one. "It's still my favorite."

Devon didn't answer. She just reached for him. Their mouths brushed, and he nibbled on her lower lip, touched with his tongue. Savored her essence, drowning in her musky scent and satiny, damp skin. He pulled her hair over her breasts, watching how her hard nipples poked through, cherry red and edible. He licked the tips, admiring his handiwork.

Her breath came faster. Sucking firmly, his hand drifted down between her legs, sliding easily into her hot wetness. His fingers played. "God, you're so ready for me. What are you doing to me, flower girl?"

She opened her thighs and arched. "I'm blooming for you, Jameson. Take me."

He muttered a curse. Quickly donning a condom, he pushed inside her swollen heat but this time, he went slow. Every thrust was measured. He drank in every flicker of her expression, adjusting his movements and speed based on her features, until he had her at the edge.

Then he kept her there. Her pleas were prayers to his ears. Her body was his to worship. And when he was about to break apart himself, Jameson dug his fingers into her hips and pulled her up, taking her hard and deep until she screamed his name and came all over his dick, her body jerking in his arms, giving herself up and over to him.

He took his own release with the last jarring thought screaming through his mind.

He was never letting this go.

He was never letting her go.

Chapter Eleven

"Can you meet me at the shop in an hour?" she asked excitedly. Her nose was already pressed to the chilly window pane. "I want to take a walk with you."

His chuckle was like rough gravel over the phone. "Why? It's freezing and we're getting snow."

"Exactly! It's going to snow, Jameson, and I don't want to miss a moment."

The pause held weight. "Sweetheart, this is Jersey, not the South. You see snow all the time. In New York, we all dread it."

"We're by the ocean so it usually doesn't stick here. We get rain and mud and sleet, but rarely snow. This is going to be an old-fashioned storm. Will you walk in the snow with me?"

"Yes, flower girl. I will. Dress warm. Be there soon with Bear."

She laughed with glee and rushed upstairs to change. The morning had been nonstop with a Sunday event, and new client bookings, but it was 4pm and she was done for the day. Brunch was over at Vintage so Jameson had the time and Devon was going to make the most of it.

She donned fur lined leggings, a sweater, and boots. Pulling on a red knit hat and scarf, she finished up and waited outside. The sky looked like a cranky toddler ready to shed tears. The ocean roared in grey, moody fury. She glanced up and down the empty streets where everything was locked up tight, lights were off, and most of the residents and businesses had closed up and gone home.

Perfect.

He arrived a few minutes later with Bear clipped to a leash. Her gaze appreciated the expensive black ski jacket, tight wool pants, and Timberland boots. A charcoal knit hat that matched his eyes was pulled low on his brow. She touched the square of leather imprinted on the side that was stitched with a pattern of dots. "What's that?"

"Braille. I got this from a company called Two Blind Brothers. They both have a disease where they lost their central vision and opened up their own store. I like the stuff there, and all proceeds go to research. A close friend of mine's son has Starguard disease and lost his sight at only sixteen. It was a lot for the family to handle."

Her fingers caressed his smooth cheek and coasted over his soft lips. "I'm sorry, that's terrible."

His eyes flickered with pain. "Sometimes, you wake up one day and go to bed a different person. You never know what's coming." She allowed him the silence, but then he shook his head with a smile. "Sorry, I got distracted. Let's go and walk in this amazing snowstorm. If it ever starts."

He tucked her arm in his and they headed to the boardwalk. They passed the empty, winding beach paths and listened to the roar of the waves as they crashed over the sand. The salt air whipped in warning, and she snuggled into his warmth, enjoying the wild open sky above and the deserted space around them. Bear trotted happily, his thick fur the perfect protection, snapping at the slowly drifting snowflakes that were beginning to fall.

They walked and chatted for a while. Jameson paused in front of an empty storefront near the arcade and peered in. Old signs and construction equipment filled the raw space. "Another ice cream place?" he asked. "Can anyone manage more ice cream in Cape May?"

She laughed. "Hey, we take our ice cream seriously here. Actually, this used to be a clothes shop, then a sandwich place, but it closed during Covid. The deal with the soft serve place fell through so I heard Davis is trying to fill it. He's the one who rents out this strip of businesses."

"Hmm." He stared inside for a while. "It used to be a casual restaurant?"

"Yeah, like sandwiches, hamburgers, and hot dogs. There's too many of them around so it never caught on with the tourists. There's even a patio in the back that overlooks the beach, which was a nice feature, but makes the price steep."

"Hmm."

She leaned her head against his shoulder. Bear sniffed around the edges of the building and peed. "What are you thinking?"

"That it's interesting. Seems like there's a lot of five-star restaurants around here. Too much competition, you think?"

"Not for the summer season. I think to do well, you need to cultivate a stellar reputation for food and service, then the people will come. But you also have to accept you'll make a lot less money off season."

"Hmm. What do other businesses do to meet expenses? Any idea?"

"You need to cater to the locals off-season. Mad Batter does very well here, and so do a few others. Beach front is a bit harder to pull off in the winter though. You'd need to offer something unique to keep the locals coming back. That's always the challenge."

"Hmm."

"You're a deep thinker, huh?"

He bumped her shoulder playfully. "I am. There's a lot going on in my head."

"That's sexy."

He laughed and kissed her. The snow began to fall harder, swirling around them and dancing in the fierce wind. She tilted her head up and breathed deep, treasuring this perfect moment in time, in a snowstorm, in a home she loved, with her dog and the man she was falling in love with.

It was silly. A bit ridiculous. Way past her comfort zone.

But there was nothing she could do about it.

She was falling in love with Jameson Franklin.

What a mess.

His phone rang and he fished it out of his pocket. "Sorry, sweetheart, I gotta take this. It's Mac."

"Of course."

He lifted the phone to his ear. "Hey, buddy. How's it going?"

Devon took the leash and led Bear toward the beach, giving Jameson some privacy. She pondered this new revelation of her feelings. He'd warned her this could get messy. She just hadn't counted on such intense emotion for the man so quickly. He was like this winter storm-- starting with a touch of grumpiness and distrust, gaining slow speed and confidence, then falling to catch her in an embrace with such grace and beauty she had no choice but to surrender.

What was she going to do?

Jameson lived in the city. He loved his job, and worked endless hours. There was no time for a long-distance relationship, and she was afraid if they tried, they'd end up tearing each other apart. Did they have enough between them for her to move to New York if he asked? She could work in a floral shop near him. Or see if she wanted to start her own business there. She loved Cape May with her heart and soul, but he may be more important. She'd never loved like this before so she didn't know the rules. But if she mentioned any of this, he may think she was being ridiculous talking so seriously after three weeks.

Maybe she was.

Devon played with Bear until he got off the phone. His back was turned from her as he deposited the cell back in his jacket pocket. She walked toward him.

"Mac's okay, I hope?"

His voice sounded a bit funny. "Actually, he's doing really good. He's ecstatic. She had the baby—a healthy boy. Five pounds one ounce. Named him Broderick."

Devon tilted her head, trying to understand why he didn't seem happy. "That's great news! His sister is good? No issues?"

"Nope. Delivery was fine, they gave her a C-section, but she'll heal fast. Even better? Her husband will be coming next week—he was able to get orders home earlier than expected."

"This is wonderful." He wouldn't look at her. She stared at his profile, as if carved in stone, and tried not to feel sick. "What's the matter, Jameson? Why don't you seem like this is a good thing?"

Slowly, he turned his head to look at her. She sucked in her breath at the gravity in his winter gaze; the storm of emotion threatening to escape. "I'm pleased for him, of course. But this presents a wrinkle I didn't expect so soon."

Devon realized the issue immediately. She'd just been in denial.

"Mac is coming home. Which means I'll be leaving."

The words fell hard between them. The snowfall picked up in response, and the last bit of light died away, leaving them in shadows. She didn't know what to say or how to act. She didn't know how to do anything, so she just nodded and took his hand again, and led him to her home.

They settled Bear in and closed the bedroom door.

She stepped into his arms and he kissed her, and for a while, they forgot the rest and focused on each other.

* * * *

They snuggled deep under the blankets, tangled together. His hand was in her hair. Her lips were pressed to his chest. The musky scent of sex filled the air. Moonlight trickled through the window. He was caught between waking and sleep, more deeply content than he'd ever imagined.

Her voice was whisper soft. "Jameson?"

"Yes, flower girl?"

"Has your heart ever been broken by a woman?"

The pain lanced as sharp as ever, but this time, the memory it left was softer, the edges blurred. He turned over the images in his mind and his body didn't stiffen up. The wound had begun to close when he wasn't looking, or maybe Devon had allowed it to heal by showing him something beautiful.

He rubbed the tat with his thumb absently and told the truth. "Yes. It almost destroyed me."

He heard her sharp intake of breath. It seemed impossible, but she melted into him, as if seeking to give all of her heat and life and emotion to him. "Do you think you'd ever try again?"

The question was fair. Before her, he'd have to give the truth, which was a resounding no. He never wanted to hurt like that again. It had been almost feral, the grief too black and consuming to fight from. The tattoo was his daily reminder.

But it was before he met Devon.

Jameson sensed she waited for his answer with an open mind. They didn't have much time left with each other before decisions needed to be made. It would be perfectly reasonable for him to simply give her a neutral answer and see what happened between them.

But Devon wouldn't fall apart if a committed love was something he couldn't give now. Maybe she'd wait. Maybe she wouldn't. But he loved the sheer independence of the woman lying beside him. She was strong enough to handle his truth and allow him to lean on her, whether she liked his answer or not. The women before had run, finding the wait not worth the risk. But Devon gave him a freedom to be who he was without apology.

"I think so," he said.

The idea of trying to be more with her should have struck terror. Instead, he only felt the stir of possibility. And more.

As if knowing his thoughts, Devon rolled over in one smooth motion and pinned him beneath her. Inch by slow inch, she sinuously slipped down his body, her mouth dropping hot kisses over his bare chest, abs, hips. He hissed out a breath when her breath fluttered over his erection, straining toward her in desperation.

She lifted her gaze to his.

Jameson shuddered. "I think so," he repeated, staring into her beautiful moss green eyes.

"Then show me," she whispered, right before she opened her mouth and took him deep inside.

His hand fisted in her hair. With each swipe of her tongue, he died a little. She was a goddess, a witch, a fantasy, as she sucked him hard and tight, then moved her head in a steady rhythm that drove him right to the edge.

She kept him there.

Time stopped. He chanted her name. He fought for control.

Vision blurred, he tugged her up, and watched as she straddled him. With swift motions, she slid on the condom, then sunk down on top of him.

He blistered out a curse. She wriggled her hips, taking him deeper, and arched backwards. Her hair streamed wildly down her back, to her moving hips. He cupped her breasts and watched her ride him, wondering if he'd ever be sane again.

She squeezed his dick so hard and tight he almost lost it, but she felt too good and he didn't want to rush. A cry broke from her throat, and he kept his gaze locked on hers, knowing what she needed.

"Come for me."

He reached between them and rubbed over the throbbing bud. Once. Twice.

She came.

His name raked across his ears. With a primitive roar, he unleashed with rough strokes and released. His mind blanked to nothing and allowed his heart to scream the truth as loud as her name broke from his lips.

He didn't think.

He knew.

After three weeks, he was in love with Devon Pratt.

He just didn't know what he was going to do about it.

Chapter Twelve

Devon finished arranging a dozen centerpieces for an upcoming bridal shower at Peter Shields Inn, hoping the bright florals cut through the dismal day. The snow had come and gone, leaving cold, wet slush behind. Everyone was still recovering from the holidays and wanted to hibernate, which suited her perfectly fine.

All she wanted was to spend time with Jameson. For the first time, she wished her calendar this week was empty so she could sit in Vintage and just be with him until he had to leave.

And he would leave.

The jarring thought took hold and settled in, like a nagging wound. They weren't in a position to declare their love and decide to be together. She wanted to tell him her feelings, but it wasn't fair. He'd only feel pressure, and that was the last thing she wanted.

She kept thinking about the tattoo. Carved into his wrist as a reminder for him not to try again. What was her name? What was their story? She refused to ask, sensing there were still walls built around his heart that needed a gentle, patient touch. The first time she'd realized it was a rose, the pain had hit hard, but she knew his past had nothing to do with her. Devon had to be brave and allow him his own choices. He'd either take another chance with her.

Or not.

But she also refused to deny the reality. She loved him and yes, it had happened fast, but it didn't scare her. The mechanics were the hard part, but it was also about how much he was willing to give or compromise. It seemed the woman who had broken his heart had done a real hatchet job. Simmering resentment burned inside for justice. Devon bet he was broken up with around Christmas and that's what made him hate the holiday. It made perfect sense from his previous words hinting that something had happened he wanted to forget.

Jealousy pricked, which was ridiculous. She was his past. A nameless, faceless ghost that could only hurt her if Devon let the memory mess with her head.

She was better than that.

Bear trotted forward as the bell tinkled and alerted him to a new guest. He'd been flourishing except for his issue with other dogs. When Devon walked him and they spotted another canine, she had to cross the street while Bear whined and trembled. It only made her want to cuddle him close and protect him.

Even though he was as big as her.

She heard Judith's greeting and made her way to the front. "Look at him, he's massive now!" the sanctuary owner exclaimed, rubbing his head. "He looks great, Devon. How is everything going?"

"Really good. He goes back and forth with Jameson and I and seems to like it. He's better on the leash and we're working on the damage control." She pointed at the chewed-up doorway to the back where Bear had happily created a new bone out of the wall. "Jameson has been working with him on the command down, so he stops jumping."

Judith nodded, but her gaze probed, full of curiosity. "This thing with Jameson seems to be going well?"

Devon smiled. "Yes."

"I'm so happy for you both," she said. Rubbing Bear's saggy, drooly jowls, the woman never flinched, obviously used to every good and bad part about having dogs. "You deserve it, Devon. A man to make you happy. I'm not sure you know how much you're cherished in this town."

Devon blinked, touched. "Thanks, Judith. That means a lot."

"It's the truth. But I'm actually here to talk about Bear and his upcoming options. I heard Mac is returning?"

Her throat tightened but she kept her tone happy. "Yes, isn't it wonderful? He plans to come home late next week."

"And will Jameson be going back to New York? Or sticking around in Cape May for a while?"

She shifted her feet. "Leaving. He has to go back to his job."

"Of course. Well, I wanted to talk about Bear's options. I know he needs some behavioral work, don't you darling?" she said, scratching Bear behind the ears. His tail wagged and he almost knocked over one of the displays, which Devon caught right in time. "He's a lot for a regular foster to handle and I appreciate you and Jameson stepping in. But this was a temporary arrangement, and I finally found something permanent for

Bear."

Her stomach clenched. "A family?"

"No, as I said, this breed is difficult to place. But a friend of mine runs a shelter in Rhode Island and knows this breed well. They have an excellent behaviorist and room so Bear will be transferred over."

"What? Wait—when?"

"End of next week." Judith's eyes held warm sympathy. "Devon, I know you've gotten attached, most temporary fosters do. You were able to give Bear a home when he didn't have one, and he will never forget you. But he needs to be in a place where he can have a permanent place, and this is the best option."

"What if I adopt him?" she rushed out.

Her words were kind but firm. "I couldn't approve it. Your place is too tiny. He can't keep staying in the floral shop all day and in a small apartment. He needs more space, and he needs to be able to deal with his issues."

"What if Mac takes him? He likes it over there and we can have the same arrangement? Mac loves dogs."

"I already spoke with Mac," she said. "He knows about Bear and right now, he doesn't want to take on the responsibility of a full-time dog. He sees more traveling in his future. He's always willing to help temporarily but Bear needs more. I'm sorry, Devon. I know how this hurts, but it's for the best."

She fought back ridiculous tears for a dog she'd never expected to love so much. But she knew Judith was right. This wasn't the right place for Bear. Not now.

Devon managed to nod. "I understand."

Judith squeezed her arm. "I know you do. I'll leave you both. You'll talk to Jameson?"

"Of course."

She gave Bear one last pat and disappeared.

Devon sunk to her knees and Bear flopped to his side for belly rubs, having no idea things were about to change.

For all of them.

* * * *

Jameson waited for her.

He sat on the couch with Bear at his feet. He'd gotten done early and everything was ready and prepped for Mac. He was proud of what he'd accomplished with Vintage and knew his cousin would be thrilled. He'd be stepping into a renovated, better organized restaurant, ready to turn a larger profit.

His sock was wet from Bear's drool. He looked around at the chewed-up furniture and endless dog hair. It should be a good thing he wouldn't have to worry about taking care of the beast, or dealing with his ridiculous issues of dog fear. He'd have more time again. Less chaos.

Less mess.

So, why did the thought of losing Bear feel close to grief?

He'd gotten used to him over the past month. Funny, the time seemed so short until you dealt with the mystery of emotions. How can someone fall in love with a dog so quickly?

How can someone fall in love with a woman without years of dating?

Yet, it had happened. He couldn't tell her, of course. He had to go back to New York, but he needed Devon to know this was all real. She wasn't a fling, a transitional, or a temporary affair. She was a woman he cared deeply about, and wanted to see if it was possible to work it out long distance.

He heard the gentle knock at the door and then she let herself in. Quietly, she sat down next to him on the couch and wrapped her arms around him. They sat together for a while, comfortable in the silence, happy with Bear and the feeling of being close.

"I know it's the right thing," he finally said. "I just don't want to give him up."

He pressed his forehead to hers and stroked back her silky hair. Her legs bent at the knee and were draped over his thighs. Her breath was warm and minty, rushing over his lips. "Neither do I. I wish there was another option but I can't think of one."

"This got messy," he said.

Her lips twitched in a smile. He cupped her cheek. "Do you regret it?"

"Never."

Her body melted into his and he kissed her, slow and deep. "What do you want to do?" she asked when he pulled away.

"Keep seeing you. Figure it out. I care too much to walk away."

"Me, too."

He didn't tell her he loved her. He didn't tell her he wished he could buy a big ass house and move her and Bear in. That just wasn't reasonable. So, he gave her something else, something he hadn't shared with anyone.

"I haven't let myself go this deep with a woman before. Not

since…her. I'd like to explain why."

He sensed her slight hesitation, as if she was afraid to hear what he had to say. But when she tipped her head back and met his gaze, he only saw warm empathy and an invitation to hold his secrets with care. "I'd like to hear it."

"It was my mother." She sucked in her breath but remained silent. "My dad was never in the picture so my mom was everything to me. And we were really close. It was funny, when all my friends used to complain about their moms all up in their business, and how frustrated they were, I never understood. It was like we just got each other, it was us against the world. I went to college for food service and management. I graduated at the top of my class and she was there every step of the way. Sure, I wished many times I had a dad in the picture, but she gave me so much, there was never any lack in my life."

Devon took his hands and squeezed tight. The warm pressure gave him a sense of peace as he continued. "We used to go to different restaurants and created a book of our favorite meals and places to go. Never once did she question my decisions, even if I made the wrong one. She'd just be there to support me when my life blew up. And damn, it happened a lot."

They smiled at each other, and he looked at her beloved face, realizing it had been a long time since he spoke about his mom. It felt good to share, as if breathing fresh air into a damp, musty closet.

"One day, she told me she found a lump in her breast and needed surgery. She made it sound easy, like they'd take it out and she'd be fine. But then they discovered it had spread. She went through chemo." He clenched his jaw, fighting the awful images of his mom struggling so hard not to leave him. "It didn't work."

The raw empathy in her gaze steadied him. Her emotion eased some of the ache in his chest, like she was releasing something he couldn't himself. "She died three days before Christmas. I remember looking at the lights and the decorated tree. I listened to the carolers and everyone around me with their joy and enthusiasm over a holiday, and kept thinking over and over that I'd lost my mother. How could the world be happy when my mom was gone? It seemed like a cruel joke. Took me years to even be able to stand any of the trappings. I went to a grief counselor because I was in a bad place for a very long time. Lost jobs. Drank a lot." He dragged in a breath. "I didn't want that. Mom would have been devastated to know I was ruining my life, so I took time and worked on myself to get better. But the sting of Christmas has always been a hurdle for me. Brings it all back."

Slowly, she picked up his hand, turning his palm up. His skin tingled as she caressed his tattoo. "What was your mother's name?" she asked softly.

His heart stopped, then thundered. "Rose. Her name was Rose."

She nodded and bent her head, brushing her lips over the ink. His skin was wet when she looked at him. He brushed her tears away, touched at her naked emotion; by her being able to share his grief. "I'm sorry, Jameson. So much makes sense now."

"Devon, this past Christmas we spent together? It was the first time I felt good again. That's what you bring to me." He paused and looked in her eyes. "Hope."

She wrapped him in her arms, laid her head on his heart, and held him for a long, long time.

Chapter Thirteen

"Good to see you, man. How was the trip?" Jameson greeted his cousin in the parking lot of the Physick Estate.

Mac gave him a short, hard hug. "Pretty damn nice. Flew business class on my sister's dime. Watched a bunch of movies and slept decent. Is that what the good life is like?" he teased.

Jameson laughed, knowing his cousin loved to rib him about being a big time, fancy New Yorker at a starred French restaurant. "Welcome to my world. In fact, I have a huge surprise for you. I'm glad you were able to come straight here."

Mac rubbed his hands together. "Are you kidding? I miss this place big time. Vintage is in my blood. How did everything work out? I heard there were a few bumps with the Fur Gala but it ended up being a huge success."

He paused, wondering how much to tell his cousin, but he figured the gossip zinging around town already hinted at his experiences here. No need to go into more detail. Jameson was slated to return to work on Monday. Usually, diving into the chaos and stress of the restaurant he'd learned to love would stir excitement. It was a familiar world for the past five years, and he never questioned his happiness with the choice.

Until now.

Shaking off his thoughts, he forced a smile. "Yep, we worked out all the kinks and it was a great event."

"Glad to hear it. And Devon? She's an amazing woman. I heard you two have gotten close."

"Yeah, we have."

Mac cocked his head and studied his face. "And? Is it serious? Are you going to keep seeing her?"

The question burned in his gut because the answer sucked. Yes, but he hated the idea of fitting her in around his crazed schedule. "We're working it out," he said.

Mac got the message and dropped the subject. "Great. So, what's the surprise?"

"Let's just say I made some changes." Mac raised a brow. "I think you'll find a different Vintage than what you left behind."

"That's mysterious."

"Come on, follow me."

Jameson led him down the winding path and through the back. After the storm, the weather turned mild again, so customers chose to eat out on the covered patio with the heaters. It was the lull between brunch and dinner so the place was deserted.

Mac stopped on the edge of the path and stared. "Where are all the lights?"

"Got rid of them. Gave the place an upgrade. Some of that stuff was years old and outdated. I ordered new linens and settings to bring in a bit of elegance to the casual atmosphere. The colors were faded so I went with a neutral gray and offset purple for a bit of contrast. See how sleek it looks?"

Mac didn't respond. He prowled around the patio, looking around, trying to take it all in. Excitement stirred. Finally, all his hard work would pay off when Mac saw all the amazing changes. "Your liquor license wasn't being used appropriately so I hired a bartender, upgraded the liquor and wine choices, and put in mimosa and bloody mary specials on Sundays."

Mac blinked. "I have a bar?"

Jameson clapped him on the shoulder with delight. "That's right. With a sixty percent markup! How's that for profit?"

No answer. Mac seemed a bit confused so Jameson led him to the main dining area. "You'll see I re-arranged the tables to fit more—people don't mind sitting close to one another so I squeezed in five more. More customers, more profit. The new rug and centerpieces allow for a more streamlined space."

Trisha walked in and lit up when she saw Mac. "You're back! I'm so happy! How's your sister and the baby?"

"Everyone's good. I'll bore you with pics later." A frown creased his brow. "Why are you dressed like that? All in black?"

Trisha glanced over. Her tone was neutral. "Jameson got us new uniforms."

"I see." Mac nodded. "I'll talk to you later, okay? I'm getting the big tour."

"Good luck," Trisha muttered, hurrying away.

Jameson shook his head. "Your staff is great, Mac, but they really took advantage. I was able to get them on an organized shift schedule by denying most of their requests. I think you'll find less turnover now. And the uniforms keep everyone on the same level. You need consistency at a restaurant—not servers displaying their own personal style everywhere. Right?"

No answer. Jameson figured his cousin was in shock. Pride weaved through him "The menu is brand-new and I think you'll love it. Very classy and fresh. Very beach town like but with a twist. Here." He handed it over and Mac glanced over it, turning away.

Silence settled over the room.

"I know it's a lot to take in, but honestly? It was my pleasure to do it. You've always given so much to others it's hard to watch people take advantage of you. Sure, there were some bumps in the road with people getting used to things, but I didn't mind at all. What do you think?"

Jameson waited for his cousin to get emotional. To hug him and thank him and confess he'd been worried about Vintage and now it had been saved. He puffed up his chest, ready to accept the gratitude in a manly, humble manner. Because it was true. He'd done all of it so Mac could have a more profitable, organized restaurant.

Slowly, Mac spun around, his face full of shock, his dark eyes glittering with...

Anger.

"Jameson, what the hell did you do to my restaurant?"

He blinked. "What do you mean? I made it better. For you."

A curse blistered the air. Mac dragged a hand through his hair, obviously pissed off. "No, you didn't, dude. You made it worse. Why did you open a bar? And why is my staff in boring ass uniforms?" He clenched his jaw and jabbed a finger at him. "And where the hell is the pancake charcuterie board on my menu?"

"I-I changed things to make you more money! I thought Vintage was a bit dated and old, so I gave it a refresh. Look how sleek and classic it looks now. There's brand new linens and flatware and décor. There's mimosas and lobster tacos. The staff and the town stopped taking advantage. I did this all for you!"

The silence was shattering. Mac shook his head and stared at him with a look of deep disappointment. "No, you didn't," he finally said quietly. "You did it for yourself. You made Vintage into your restaurant and now I have to clean up the mess."

"But—"

He put out a hand. "Don't. I need some time to talk to my staff and see what I'm going to do. I'll meet you at the house later."

"Mac—"

But his cousin had already marched away.

Jameson glanced around the place, his insides churning with a mass of rage, shock, and bitterness. How could Mac say that? All Jameson's hard work and sweat and pulling in big contacts had been done to make things better, and this was his thank you? His cousin stalking off and blaming him?

The hell with this.

He left Vintage, frustration nipping at his heels with every step. *Screw it. He was going home where he belonged.*

* * * *

Devon walked into Vintage and spotted Mac.

Bear got ready to leap in greeting but with a firm pull and command, he sat back on his haunches. He was so smart. A burst of pride filled her until she remembered the dog wasn't theirs.

Hers and Jameson's.

Devon smiled as Mac walked over. He looked a bit stressed, but that would be expected returning from a month away. "Welcome back," she greeted. "Congrats on the new member of your family."

"Thanks. Good to see you. Is this the famous Bear who's been living in my house?"

"This is the one. There may be a few repairs needed," she said with a wince.

He laughed and rubbed his head. "I'm not worried about it." They chatted a bit about his sister and trip. "Are you here to see Jameson?"

"Yes, he texted me before and said we'd meet here. Is he around?"

"He left."

The words were thrown out like stones and landed hard and swift. "Okay. Is he at your house?"

Mac let out a frustrated breath. His features tightened with emotion. "Don't know. We had an issue."

Devon paused, not knowing whether to pry in family business. Then again, she loved Mac's cousin. "Can I assume you weren't happy with the changes he made?" she asked gently.

"You assume right." He muttered a curse. "What the hell was he thinking? Why would he believe changing my restaurant while I was away could possibly be a good idea? This place reeks of his style and vision, not mine. Not the town's and my customers I've served for years. He had no right."

She bit her lip, not surprised at Mac's reaction. Jameson had stubbornly refused to see what she'd tried to tell him, but she also understood now he'd done it out of love. Yes, he'd screwed up. Yes, he'd given Mac the restaurant he dreamed of creating, and had gotten blurred by his ambition. But Devon knew he'd meant to help. "I agree. I tried to warn him. We all did. But I've learned your cousin is a bit muleheaded when he believes something is right."

Mac gave a half laugh. "Runs in the family."

"I bet." She sighed, trying to find the right way to explain. "Mac, I don't blame you for being pissed. He should have communicated with you and listened to what you wanted. But I think he saw a way he could help his family and his intentions were good. He just got lost along the way."

"Yeah, I know. It was just a shock, I needed to process." He groaned. "I've got a lot of work to put things back in order around here."

"Don't be too hard on him."

He studied her, his expression registering surprise. "Holy crap. You love him."

She jerked back and almost fell on her ass. "Huh?"

"It's all over your face. I should've known this was bigger than a fling. Jameson is married to his work—he's not the type to get sidetracked by a holiday romance unless it was special. What are you guys going to do?"

She didn't even bother with denial. "He'll go back to New York. We'll try to do the long-distance thing and work it out. Just don't tell him how I feel, okay?"

"I won't. But you should. It changes things."

A sad smile curved her lips. "Exactly. I don't want him to feel pressure to say it back, or feel he's leading me on."

"Jameson's not like that. But it's between you and I won't get involved. I'll talk to him later about this and straighten things out."

"Thanks. I'll see you later."

She headed out with Bear and wondered if Jameson would decide to leave earlier now that Mac wasn't happy about the surprise. But she had no control over what happened next.

Like Peter Pan said, all she could do was have faith and trust that what they had together could sustain distance and hurdles.

But damn, she wouldn't mind a bit of pixie dust for luck.

Chapter Fourteen

Jameson walked.

In New York, when he needed to calm down after a stressful night at the restaurant, he'd walk the streets for hours. Sometimes, he'd be early enough to watch the bakeries open and smell the fresh bread. Sometimes, he'd head to the river by the fish market and watch the organized chaos as vendors bought supplies, himself included. He'd become an expert in recognizing the freshest seafood for the best prices. It was a cutthroat and ruthless industry, but he'd become a part of it and flourished.

He never imagined himself anywhere else, but after a month in Cape May, doubts were beginning to creep in. He loved being by the ocean, even in winter. He'd begun to love watching the familiar customers at Vintage, even when they complained, and learning about their lives. He enjoyed Mac's large house with plenty of space and a yard, even though the décor was awful.

And he'd begun to love Bear, even though he wasn't a dog person.

Things had changed. But once he returned to his life, would he miss this, or forget? Was this like living in a bubble of Camelot, yet destined to remain almost a dream?

His instincts roared no. Devon was more. She was his Guinevere, and he was…

Well, not Lancelot. Probably more like the King. Too invested in his knights at the round table to give enough romance to Guinevere.

Ah, hell, he was losing his mind. Why was he suddenly casting them as roles in a tragic romance story?

Not caring about his shoes, he walked onto the beach and stood by the ocean. The salt air rose to his nostrils. The sky was gray and wintry. The water looked cold and dark and depressing. But the pull of the waves and the endless stretch of sand around him settled his mind and his heart.

There was magic here, in this little beach town. It called to him.

Like Devon.

But he couldn't change his life after a few weeks with someone. Plus, the first half had begun with them disliking each other. He needed to be rational, even though his heart throbbed with the simple knowledge he'd found his person.

He stood on the sand and thought for a while. The thing with Mac had completely thrown him off. He kept going over all the things he'd done and couldn't understand why Mac was so upset. Because he felt embarrassed Jameson had done better? No, that wasn't like his cousin. Did he feel like Jameson was trying to take over and felt threatened? Again, not like Mac. Something didn't fit.

The memory of his words stung.

You made Vintage into your own restaurant.

You did it for you.

Bullshit. He'd never do that.

Right?

He didn't want his own restaurant. At least, he never had before. Sure, being at Vintage gave him a different perspective and the idea had tickled his brain a bit. But Mac was being unfair with is accusations.

Jameson walked to the boardwalk and passed the vacant store space. He stopped and took his time examining the inside. His mind spun with possibilities and questions. Taking out his phone, he typed in the number for the realtor. Wouldn't hurt to see what the rent was like around here. Maybe he'd research the competition. Get an idea of what places succeeded, what didn't, and why.

Maybe.

When his thoughts calmed, he texted Dev that he'd meet her at the shop.

It was time to talk.

* * * *

They lay in the bed, wrapped up in each other. Devon tried to focus on the present instead of the future. Soon, he'd be gone, and she needed to adjust to life without him here. She wasn't about to ruin her happiness with what-ifs and unknown tomorrows. Sometimes, the moment needed to be enough.

"You're leaving Sunday?"

"Yeah. I'll have to pack up my stuff early morning. I need time to get re-settled and into work on Monday."

She hooked her leg over his ankle, rubbing her calf over his hair-roughened skin. "Are you looking forward to getting back to your kingdom?"

He chuckled, absently stroking her hair. "Sure. I think I'm still off about the Mac thing. I need to talk to him."

"I'm sure you'll work it out."

He turned his head and held her gaze. "You knew the whole time, didn't you? That he'd hate it."

She pressed her lips together. "I did tell you."

"Yeah, you did. I guess I thought the bigger vision of Vintage was what he wanted.."

"There's nothing wrong with trying to help family, Jameson. I just think you got tangled up with your own dreams without realizing it."

He didn't speak for a while, and his soothing motions lulled her into relaxation. "Maybe you're right, flower girl. I do know since I met you, everything I believed is suddenly in question."

"I won't apologize for that, restaurant boy."

"Don't want you to."

"So, we agree to take this long distance and see what happens?"

He cupped her chin and pressed his forehead to hers. "Yes. Because I—" he cut himself off, swallowing his next words. She searched his gaze for the truth but the raw flicker of emotion had been firmly banked. "I care about you."

She took what he gave her and pushed down her own confession. "I care about you, too."

Then he kissed her and they were silent for a long time.

Two days later, he'd be gone.

* * * *

Jameson got dressed and left Devon sleeping. Bear perked up and trotted after him, squeezing into the small kitchen while he made coffee. "Don't shake your head, beast. You'll get hair in my mug."

Bear pulled back his drooly lips and grinned.

He laughed, patting him on his giant head that had crashed through Mac's screen door last week. Guess he'd believed it was open, so Jameson would take the blame on that one. He fed him breakfast and fresh water, which was gobbled up in seconds. "Ready?"

Bear wagged his tail and bounded to the door, wriggling his butt.

Jameson clipped on his leash and they headed out.

They walked in companiable silence, content with their morning routine. Jameson liked his time with Bear now. It was as if he was able to connect with another part of himself with the dog that he'd never known existed. But it was time to have the talk so he stopped at a bench to sit and Bear obediently sat beside him.

"I'm leaving Sunday to go back to New York, beast. And you're going to a new place, too, on Monday. You may get nervous and you may not like it at first. Change is hard, believe me. But I know the people at the shelter—Judith and Devon—they know what's best. You need space and can't be cooped up in a New York loft with me gone all the time. And Devon's apartment is the same, it's not fair to you."

Jameson studied the dog's face. Bear cocked his head, seeming to listen.

"I really didn't like you at first. I'm not a dog person. But you won me over. You're a good dog, Bear. And I'm really going to miss you, more than you know."

Those big, soulful brown eyes stared into his, and Jameson imagined there was understanding there.

And love.

His throat tightened. "That's it. Wanna take a dump in that weed spot you like?"

Bear jumped up, ready to go.

"Yeah, it's a good place. Come on."

Jameson led him to the spot and realized saying goodbye really sucked.

Hours later, he met with Mac. He'd already packed up his things and loaded the car. He faced his cousin in the living room, surrounded by the cheap tacky knickknacks and worn furniture and beach happiness and began to see more of his cousin's heart and soul than he had before.

"You still pissed?" he asked.

Mac shot him a look. "A little. But it won't last. Listen, dude, you screwed up. You should've called me and told me your plan. I would've told you Vintage is perfect the way it is. I like the BYOB and the pancakes and the staff giving me shit. The customers like the vibe. I don't need fancy or a profit. I need to be exactly what I am--happy."

Jameson winced. "Yeah, I wasn't thinking like that. I'm sorry, Mac. I have all this knowledge from years in the business and I saw something really big for you. I just wanted to help."

"That's why I forgive you. Devon said the same thing when we spoke."

"She didn't tell me." The thought of Devon defending him threw him off. Pleasure and longing crashed within, dragging him over the sand like the waves. "She was the one warning me not to do it. Said you'd hate it."

"Devon's smart. I'm glad you both got together. She's good for you. And vice versa."

He tilted his head with curiosity. "Why?"

Mac grinned. "She sees past that stick up your ass surface. Knows your heart. And you obviously treasure her in a way she's been missing."

He liked his cousin's words but it also hurt since he was leaving her behind.

Mac reached out and patted his arm. "Look, Jameson, I gotta tell you something. What you do with it is up to you. I think you'd be perfect to open up your own place. You have all the vision and knowledge and expertise to be a success. And I think you should do it right here, in Cape May, where you can be near Devon, and some family."

The words jolted him. "I've been here a month. You really think I should give up my job, my place, my friends, and my life to chase a woman I've known for a few weeks and settle in a small beach town?"

Mac laughed. "Hell, yes, I do. And that's all I'm going to say. Just…think about it. Your life can be anything you want, dude. You get to make the choices."

They said goodbye and Jameson left with his cousin's words echoing in his head.

Chapter Fifteen

Jameson smiled at the screen and wished he could touch her. "How bad was the wedding?"

She groaned and pushed her hair back. His fingers tingled at the thought of how those strands felt slipping through his fingers, like raw silk. "Bad. Poor Gabe got hit on by the bridesmaids—they were so trashed, and I thought Bella was going to tackle them to the floor in a cat fight."

"Did she?"

"God, no, she's got class. She just made out with him in front of a crowd and lifted his finger to show off his wedding band. Then walked away with her head high. They didn't bother him after that."

"That's kick ass. Would you do that for me?"

Her voice lowered in a sexy whisper. "I don't need any excuse to make out with you, restaurant boy."

He laughed, but the time on the clock was like a ticking bomb. "Sweetheart, I gotta go. I'll check in later."

"Okay, have a good shift."

He opened his mouth, then quickly shut it. It seemed so natural to tell her he loved her but he knew it was too much. "Talk later. Miss you."

"Miss you."

He clicked off and headed to his closet to change. His head whirred with images of Devon wrapped up in his arms, with Bear at their side, running a restaurant that he had an emotional stake in.

God, he was tired. The long shifts weren't invigorating anymore to him. Instead, his energy was always sapped. They'd made a change in management so now he was working with a guy in the field that was arrogant and a know-it-all. Tension was consistently simmering between them. Jameson figured a confrontation was coming soon because he couldn't have his authority questioned.

But the bottom line? The Bordeaux Café wasn't his place. He did what the bosses told him. He was a very highly paid manager. Not an owner.

The late-night dinners with his friends seemed tarnished and not as shiny or as fun. Many of them complained about the same things--their crappy hours, their toys, and work. The relationships they were in never lasted.

Jameson headed to work and thought of the beach. The flower shop. His cousin. And Bear. He thought about that vacant space and the phone number still held in his phone.

The evening went south pretty quickly. The chef overcooked the special and customer complaints flowed in. The new guy refused to defend the chef or the current staff, instead kissing ass to the customer and turning his back on his own. Jameson brought him aside to reign him in but was met with hot-tempered insults.

"That's it. You're not going to work out here. You're done," Jameson said.

Brent sneered. "You can't fire me, asshole. I'm Jacques's nephew."

Jameson stared back, shocked. He'd never been told there was a connection there. What was going on?

Brent seemed to catch on to his ignorance and gave a mocking laugh. "You don't get it, huh? I'm going to be your boss soon. So, it may help to start working with me rather than against me, or maybe it's you who's gonna be looking for another job."

Then with a nasty grin, he left.

When Jameson got home that night, stressed, overworked, and exhausted, he looked up the number. He muttered a curse and rolled up his shirt sleeves. What the hell was he doing? Blowing up his life because of one bad night? Or running to a better one?

His gaze caught on the inked rose, reminding him of Devon.

He blinked. *Devon*. Not the grief over losing his mom. Not the empty hole inside of him or the reminder of love lost. Just Devon's beautiful, kind face and the joy she brought.

His brain exploded with an image of his mom standing by Devon, smiling, enclosing her into a hug in full approval. The tattoo burned around his wrist in foreboding. What if he'd gotten this ink years ago for his future soul-mate? His very own flower girl.

What if his mother had led him directly to her?

Jameson closed his eyes and everything settled inside him. He knew exactly what he needed to do.

He called the number.

* * * *

Devon finished her final bouquet and flexed her cramped fingers. God, she loved and hated Valentine's Day. It was the most profitable day for her shop, but it was a bitch to handle. Endless parties and nonstop restaurant orders poured in. She hired an extra driver for the week to deal with the rush. Glancing at her phone, she tried to tamp down her disappointment that Jameson hadn't called.

It had been one month since he'd left. They managed to see each other twice in rushed visits. Jameson had no time off after taking leave, so he worked mostly seven days a week. The one day he'd managed to get shift coverage, he'd driven to Cape May so he could spend the night.

She thought of the weekend she'd gone to New York. It was wonderful to be in his environment and see the fancy restaurant he managed. She loved walking the streets hand in hand and spending the night in his arms. But he had little time to give, and seemed stressed out.

Devon tried not to worry. After all, this was new to them both, and Jameson was overwhelmed with his job. She was positive they could find a balance in the future. Still, this was the second time he'd missed their phone date and it was Valentine's Day. She just…missed him.

Blowing out a breath, she finished up and cleared the table. The emptiness of the shop made her ache. Bear was missed daily, but she knew the training was important for him. He deserved the best home. It just happened not to be hers.

Feeling a touch of self-pity, she went upstairs and poured herself a deserved glass of wine. Maybe she'd watch a movie tonight. No romcoms. Something with guns and violence and action to distract her.

Devon groaned at the knock on her door. Muttering under her breath, she peeked out the window.

Jameson stood at the door with dozens of roses.

She gasped and flung the door open. "What are you doing?"

"Not missing Valentine's Day, of course."

She blinked back sudden tears and bit down on her lip to steady herself. "What about work?"

"Don't care. I missed you, sweetheart."

She jumped into his arms, crushing the flowers, and his mouth met hers with hunger and fire and want. Devon melted into the embrace, frantic to get as close to him as possible. He backed her up, kicked the door shut, and they made out in her hallway until they were breathless.

When he finally broke the kiss, her entire body throbbed with arousal. "I can't believe you drove all the way here just for Valentine's Day," she murmured, gathering up the blooms with care.

"I wanted to talk to you about something."

The gravity in his voice stopped her heart. What if he came here to break up in person? What if this wasn't working for him any longer? What if she wasn't enough for him?

She tamped down on the negative thoughts and tried to remain calm. "Well, it must be important if it couldn't be done over the phone."

"It is. I couldn't wait anymore, Devon. It isn't fair to you."

She focused on clipping the stems under water and arranging the roses in a vase. "Okay." Her voice shook a bit. "What is it?"

"I think you should sit."

Her stomach clenched. She may throw up but that wasn't cool. She needed to be calm. "Okay." Slowly, she walked to the couch and sat down. Her smile seemed forced and a bit sickly. "I'm ready. What did you want to talk about?"

He paced back and forth with a restless panther grace she loved. Pushing his glasses up the bridge of his nose, a frown marred his brow. "I don't know how to say this without freaking you out. I thought about doing it over a nice dinner, or maybe over the phone because you deserved to hear it. Hell, I shouldn't have been afraid to do this before but I was worried about your reaction. But here we go."

Oh, God.

"Sweetheart, I'm really sorry but this isn't working between us. The long-distance thing, I mean."

Fuck calm, cool and collected.

She jumped from the couch. "You're breaking up with me because it's not easy for you? Because your idea of a relationship isn't what you imagined? Well, welcome to my world, restaurant boy! The difference between us is I can recognize when a connection is this rare, and real, and raw, and not throw it away because things are a little hard!"

"Devon—"

She shook with emotion, her voice breaking. "No, forget it! I'm sick and tired of trying to hide the truth. Hell, I might as well scare the hell out of you right now since you're already spooked. You see, Jameson Franklin, I happen to be in love with you. Okay? I love you, you idiot!"

His jaw dropped. "You love me?"

She despised the tears that stung her eyes but she'd lost control. "Yes. I do. And I'm not taking it back. So go ahead and break up with me, and I'm sorry I can't do this sweetly and be cool and say, hey, we tried it didn't work out, because I'm hurt, and sad, and really, really pissed off!"

And then he laughed.

He threw back his head and laughed so hard, Devon's vision blurred, and she reacted the only way she knew.

She threw herself at him in a feminine fury. "Why are you laughing! How can I love someone so stupid!"

He tightened his embrace and yanked her close. "Flower girl, you have to listen. You didn't give me a chance to finish." She stilled and he cupped her cheeks, looking into her eyes with so much heat and want and tenderness. "I love you, too. I've been miserable in New York without you, and I fell in love with you before I left but I was too scared to tell you. I kept telling myself no one can be in love after three weeks but I was wrong. I left my job, Devon. I want to move here and be with you and open up a restaurant. I want us to be a family."

The words stunned her. She gripped his shirt with trembling hands. "You—you love me? You want to move here?"

"Yes. I did a lot of thinking about what I want and realized I thought I was happier than I was. After meeting you and being in Cape May, I see there's a whole other level and I want it all. With you. Is that okay, flower girl?"

She reached up on her tiptoes and pressed her lips to his. "Yes, it's very okay. God, I love you so much."

He scooped her up into his arms and headed to the bedroom. "I hope you don't have any events tonight," he murmured, laying her out on the mattress. "Because I don't expect us to make it."

She linked her arms around his neck and sighed in pleasure. "I'm all yours."

And Jameson made good on his promise.

Epilogue

Jameson shifted his feet nervously and paced. "They're late."

"Only ten minutes. It's okay, they'll be here," Devon soothed.

He gave her a quick smile but resumed pacing. Devon went to the kitchen and came back with two seltzers, handing him one. He took a few sips, absently admiring his new place he now called home.

Mac had worked with the local realtor to get him first dibs on a two level for sale in North Cape May. It was only a ten-minute drive into town and had plenty of space, a whole acre of land, and a big ass kitchen that was a chef's dream. Painted a bright yellow with a wraparound porch, Devon's first purchase was the two rockers with yellow floral cushions.

And flowers, of course. His place was already full of gorgeous plants and blooms that made the space explode with life.

He was a few months from his big opening, ready for the summer crowd. The Bistro was going to offer a fine dining event that Cape May had never experienced. Jameson knew the menu was superb, and he'd scored a big-time chef from New York to move out here and run it.

He looked at Devon and his heart warmed. The past few months had been filled with change, but all good. He was more in love with the woman by his side every day he spent with her. She supported him every step as he pursued his dreams, and having Mac close made him feel like he held a living piece of his mother's memory.

The doorbell rang and he jumped, spilling some of the seltzer. "They're here."

Devon smiled and opened the door. "Hi, did you have trouble finding the place?"

The woman stepped in, dressed in jeans and a t-shirt, her dark hair in a casual ponytail. "No, sorry, there was traffic and we had to stop for a break."

Jameson dragged in a breath and stepped forward. "Hi, it's nice to meet you." His heart stopped as he got a good look at the familiar dog, calmly sitting next to the woman, giant tail wagging.

Their gazes met.

His voice broke. "Bear." Those big brown eyes sparked in recognition. "Welcome home, beast."

The woman who ran the shelter in Rhode Island unclipped his leash with a smile. "Go ahead, Bear. Release."

Bear raced over and into his arms. He pet the familiar fur that flew everywhere in the air, and dealt with frantic kisses that covered him in drool. His heart exploded with joy when Devon joined them in a circle.

They were together.

And they were home.

The End

* * * *

Also from 1001 Dark Nights and Jennifer Probst, discover Something Just Like This, The Marriage Arrangement, Somehow, Some Way, Searching for Mine, and Begin Again.

Sign up for the 1001 Dark Nights Newsletter
and be entered to win a Tiffany Key necklace.

There's a contest every month!

Go to www.1001DarkNights.com to subscribe.

**As a bonus, all subscribers can download
FIVE FREE exclusive books!**

Discover 1001 Dark Nights Collection Ten

DRAGON LOVER by Donna Grant
A Dragon Kings Novella

KEEPING YOU by Aurora Rose Reynolds
An Until Him/Her Novella

HAPPILY EVER NEVER by Carrie Ann Ryan
A Montgomery Ink Legacy Novella

DESTINED FOR ME by Corinne Michaels
A Come Back for Me/Say You'll Stay Crossover

MADAM ALANA by Audrey Carlan
A Marriage Auction Novella

DIRTY FILTHY BILLIONAIRE by Laurelin Paige
A Dirty Universe Novella

HIDE AND SEEK by Laura Kaye
A Blasphemy Novella

TANGLED WITH YOU by J. Kenner
A Stark Security Novella

TEMPTED by Lexi Blake
A Masters and Mercenaries Novella

THE DANDELION DIARY by Devney Perry
A Maysen Jar Novella

CHERRY LANE by Kristen Proby
A Huckleberry Bay Novella

THE GRAVE ROBBER by Darynda Jones
A Charley Davidson Novella

CRY OF THE BANSHEE by Heather Graham
A Krewe of Hunters Novella

DARKEST NEED by Rachel Van Dyken
A Dark Ones Novella

CHRISTMAS IN CAPE MAY by Jennifer Probst
A Sunshine Sisters Novella

A VAMPIRE'S MATE by Rebecca Zanetti
A Dark Protectors/Rebels Novella

WHERE IT BEGINS by Helena Hunting
A Pucked Novella

Also from Blue Box Press

THE MARRIAGE AUCTION by Audrey Carlan
Book One
Book Two
Book Three
Book Four

THE JEWELER OF STOLEN DREAMS by M.J. Rose

SAPPHIRE STORM by Christopher Rice writing as C. Travis Rice
A Sapphire Cove Novel

ATLAS: THE STORY OF PA SALT by Lucinda Riley and Harry
Whittaker

LOVE ON THE BYLINE by Xio Axelrod
A Plays and Players Novel

A SOUL OF ASH AND BLOOD by Jennifer L. Armentrout
A Blood and Ash Novel

START US UP by Lexi Blake
A Park Avenue Promise Novel

FIGHTING THE PULL by Kristen Ashley
A River Rain Novel

A FIRE IN THE FLESH by Jennifer L. Armentrout
A Flesh and Fire Novel

Discover More Jennifer Probst

Something Just Like This
A Stay Novella

Jonathan Lake is the beloved NYC mayor who's making a run for governor. His widowed status and close relationship with his daughter casts him as the darling of the press, and the candidate to beat, but behind the flash of the cameras, things are spinning out of control. It all has to do with his strait laced, ruthlessly organized assistant. Her skills and reserved demeanor are perfect to run his campaign, but her brilliant brain has become a temptation he's been fighting for too long. Can he convince her to take a chance on a long-term campaign for love or will his efforts end up in scandal?

Alyssa Block has admired the NYC mayor for a long time, but her secret crush is kept ruthlessly buried under a mountain of work. Besides, she's not his type, and office scandals are not in her job description. But when they retreat to an upstate horse farm for a secluded weekend, the spark between them catches flame, and Jonathan sets those stinging blue eyes on winning her. Can she convince him to focus on the upcoming election, or will she succumb to the sweet promise of a different future?

* * * *

The Marriage Arrangement
A Marriage to a Billionaire Novella

She had run from her demons...

Caterina Victoria Windsor fled her family winery after a humiliating broken engagement, and spent the past year in Italy rebuilding her world. But when Ripley Savage shows up with a plan to bring her back home, and an outrageous demand for her to marry him, she has no choice but to return to face her past. But when simple attraction begins to run deeper, Cat has to decide if she's strong enough to trust again...and strong enough to stay...

He vowed to bring her back home to be his wife...

Rip Savage saved Windsor Winery, but the only way to make it truly his is to marry into the family. He's not about to walk away from the only thing he's ever wanted, even if he has to tame the spoiled brat who left her legacy and her father behind without a care. When he convinces her to agree to a marriage arrangement and return home, he never counted on the fierce sexual attraction between them to grow into something more. But when deeper emotions emerge, Rip has to fight for something he wants even more than Windsor Winery: his future wife.

* * * *

Somehow, Some Way
A Billionaire Builders Novella

Bolivar Randy Heart (aka Brady) knows exactly what he wants next in life: the perfect wife. Raised in a strict traditional family household, he seeks a woman who is sweet, conservative, and eager to settle down. With his well-known protective and dominant streak, he needs a woman to offer him balance in a world where he relishes control.

Too bad the newly hired, gorgeous rehab addict is blasting through all his preconceptions and wrecking his ideals...one nail at a time...

Charlotte Grayson knows who she is and refuses to apologize. Growing up poor made her appreciate the simple things in life, and her new job at Pierce Brothers Construction is perfect to help her carve out a career in renovating houses. When an opportunity to transform a dilapidated house in a dangerous neighborhood pops up, she goes in full throttle. Unfortunately, she's forced to work with the firm's sexy architect who's driving her crazy with his archaic views on women.

Too bad he's beginning to tempt her to take a chance on more than just work...one stroke at a time...

Somehow, some way, they need to work together to renovate a house without killing each other...or surrendering to the white-hot chemistry knocking at the front door.

* * * *

Searching for Mine
A Searching For Novella

The Ultimate Anti-Hero Meets His Match...

Connor Dunkle knows what he wants in a woman, and it's the three

B's. Beauty. Body. Boobs. Other women need not apply. With his good looks and easygoing charm, he's used to getting what he wants—and who. Until he comes face to face with the one woman who's slowly making his life hell...and enjoying every moment...

Ella Blake is a single mom and a professor at the local Verily College who's climbed up the ranks the hard way. Her ten-year-old son is a constant challenge, and her students are driving her crazy—namely Connor Dunkle, who's failing her class and trying to charm his way into a better grade. Fuming at his chauvinistic tendencies, Ella teaches him the ultimate lesson by giving him a *special* project to help his grade. When sparks fly, neither of them are ready to face their true feelings, but will love teach them the ultimate lesson of all?

* * * *

Begin Again
A Stay Novella

Chloe Lake is finally living her dream. As the daughter of the governor, she's consistently in the spotlight, and after being dubbed the Most Eligible Bachelorette of NYC, both her career and personal life has exploded. Fortunately, her work as an advocate for animal welfare requires constant publicity and funding, so she embraces her role and plays for the camera—anything for the sake of her beloved rescues.

But when a big case is on the line, she's faced with the one obstacle she never counted on: the boy who broke her heart is back, and in order to gain justice, they need to work together.

Chloe swears she can handle it until old feelings resurface, and she's faced with a heartbreaking choice.

Will this time end differently—or are they destined to be only each other's first love—instead of forever?

Owen Salt fell hard for Chloe when he was a screwed-up kid in college, and spent the next years changing himself into the man his grandfather believed he was capable of. But when his career led him across the country, he knew he needed to leave the woman he loved behind. He's never forgotten her, but as the new darling of the press, now she's way out of his league. When work brings him back to fight for justice by her side, he swears he can handle it.

But he's never really gotten over his first love—and he wants one more opportunity to prove he's a man who's worthy.

Can Owen convince the woman who holds his heart to take a second chance on forever—or is it too late for them both?

For fans of Jennifer Probst's Stay series, *Begin Again* is book five in that series.

Love on Beach Avenue

The Sunshine Sisters, Book 1
By Jennifer Probst

True love is in the details for the Jersey shore's premier wedding planner in this heart-swooning series about big dreams and happy endings from *New York Times* bestselling author Jennifer Probst.

Avery Sunshine might not have a soul mate of her own, but she still believes in happily ever after—*for her clients*. Making dreams come true is her business at Sunshine Bridal, which she runs with her two sisters. When her best friend announces her engagement, Avery is thrilled to take charge of the giddy bride-to-be's big day. Less thrilling? Her best friend's arrogant and demanding brother, who just so happens to be the man of honor.

Carter Ross's first instinct: call 911. He promised to always take care of his impulsive little sister, and he honors that vow. Even if it means taking over her wedding, where he is sure Avery will fail. At best, Avery is unpredictable. At worst, if she's anything like the spitfire of a college girl he remembers, the main event could run wild.

With Avery and Carter wrestling for control, tempers heat up. So does the spark of attraction they're fighting with every kiss. As the wedding draws near, it's time to reconcile a rocky past and make a decision that could change everyone's lives. Because what they're rebelling against looks a lot like love.

* * * *

"If anyone objects to this marriage, let them speak now, or forever hold their peace."

Avery Alyssa Sunshine stood at the back of the church, her practiced gaze sweeping over the large crowd sitting in the pews. The church was small and intimate, with soaring ceilings and elaborate stained-glass windows, giving the guests a taste of old-school religion and tradition. The lilies were creamy white and bursting with bloom. The faint scent of incense hung in the air. And her bride looked perfect—from the flowing trail of her sheer lace veil to the elaborate pearl-encrusted train that filled the chancel. The bride and groom gazed at each other with evident love, their beaming faces a reminder of why she loved her job as a wedding planner.

And then it happened.

"I object." The lone male voice boomed in the air.

The crowd gasped, and the bride jerked around, china-blue eyes filled with horror.

No. No, no, no...

Dressed in a sharp black suit, the man stood up, arms extended as if in a last-minute plea, which it was. Avery glimpsed only the back of his head, his golden-blond hair a bit long and brushing the nape of his neck. "Susan, I tried to move on, but you're the only one I've ever loved. I can't let you marry him if there's still a chance for us."

For one endless, horrifying moment, everything went dead quiet. Avery froze, her mind unable to compute this disaster since it was brand new and fell under the heading of *Shit That Hasn't Happened Yet, Thank God.*

Nothing like an on-the-job education.

The bride's face turned from horror to fury. Her teeth ground together, and her perfect rosy complexion flushed dark red. "You bastard!" she hissed through the delicate veil. "You cheated on me."

Another gasp from the crowd. The priest's jaw dropped. It was like the entire church was filming a rom-com and everyone knew their lines except Avery.

Oh, hell no. This was not going to become a *Runaway Bride* situation. Not on her watch.

She whipped out her phone and sent the text her sisters dreaded: **Code Red. Code Red in the church.**

The groom dropped his future wife's hand and shot her a puzzled look. "Baby, who is this guy? Do you still have feelings for him?"

Avery shot into action, knowing there was precious time to save the wedding. Launching down the aisle in her three-inch heels, she reached the interloper in seconds, and before he could make another earth-shattering plea, she firmly yet politely placed a hand on his arm. "Sir, please come with me," she said quietly, smile pasted in place. "Let's talk about this in private."

The bride let out a distressed cry, and the sudden hushed dialogue between the bride and groom echoed from the high ceilings and bounced straight to the ears of the crowd. Right on cue, Avery's sister Bella popped out of the private room to the side of the altar and headed toward the organist. Within seconds, the beautiful strains of "Ave Maria" floated in the air, followed by the singer's soaring soprano.

Avery prayed the interloper wouldn't fight her—she didn't want to tackle the guy in the aisle—but he seemed to realize actually breaking up a wedding wasn't as much fun as in the movies. With a ducked head, he began to follow her out of the church.

Whispering soothing phrases to the cheater, she guided him into the small room where the brides are usually held before the ceremony, and shut the door behind them. She pointed to the bench. "Have a seat. I'm sorry, I didn't get your name?"

The man rubbed his head with both hands, messing up his too-long hair even more. "Ben Larson. I've known Susan since college. We promised to marry each other, but I was too young. I think we're meant to be together."

Her mind clicked through the guest list, snagged on the name, and brought up her mental notes. Ben Larson—an old friend who'd grown up with Susan, broken up with her after college, and recently reconnected. He helped out her mother, who'd pressured Susan to invite him. Was supposed to attend with his girlfriend.

Dammit. She hadn't seen a red flag on this one.

The slight scent of beer on his breath indicated he'd had a few before the ceremony. A disjointed puzzle slowly came together: Ben breaks up with his current girlfriend. Feels sentimental, maybe a bit scared over still being alone. Has too much to drink, decides to attend the wedding alone, and in a spectacular, stupid move, impulsively convinces himself he still loves Susan.

"I understand, Ben," Avery said in a warm voice. "Hang on."

Bella would have quietly taken the bride and groom aside by now to mediate a discussion. The crowd needed one last distraction to buy them some time. Quickly, Avery tapped out a text to her other sister, Taylor.

Bring in the champagne. Need five more minutes.

Avery always made sure there were a few trays of poured champagne ready to go for any crisis. It was the ultimate distraction.

Her sister texted back. **Allowed in the church?**

Don't care. Go.

Snapping her gaze away from the phone, she studied the cheating interloper in front of her. Time to de-bomb the situation. "Ben, did you and your girlfriend break up recently?"

A ragged sigh. His lips curved downward in a bit of a sulk. "Well, yeah, but that has nothing to do with this."

"I think it does. Don't you think if you had these feelings for Susan, you would have said something sooner? Maybe it's not Susan you truly miss. Maybe it's..." She trailed off, looking for help.

"Melissa?"

"Yes, Melissa. You see, Susan always considered you a good friend, especially to her mother. She appreciates that relationship, but never believed you were meant to be together. Now, Melissa, I bet she was a better match. It must've been hard losing her."

He nodded, looking miserable. "Yeah, it was. I got scared. Was afraid she'd end up hurting me, so I broke up with her first. Stupid, huh?"

"Sometimes we do stupid things because we're afraid. But I think if you're brave enough to stand up in church and proclaim your feelings, you're brave enough to go after Melissa. The one you truly love." She paused for a beat. "Don't you?"

He looked up. His eyes sparked with a hint of determination. "Yeah, I do. You're right. I gotta get her back."

"I agree." Already, she was on her phone, getting an Uber to the front of the church. "A black SUV will be out front to take you where you need. To take you to Melissa."

"I have my car."

She shook her head. "No, you've had a few beers, and you want to make sure you practice your speech on the way over. Now, come with me. We'll go out the side door."

"Thanks." Worry flickered over his face. "Hey, I didn't mess up Susan's wedding or anything, did I? Can you tell her I made a mistake? That I love Melissa instead?"

"Of course, I'll fix it. Off you go."

She pushed him out the door and dragged in a breath. Smoothing her hair, she composed herself, reentered the church, and assessed the situation.

Guests happily sipping champagne while the soloist kept singing her heart out.

Bride and groom smiling at each other again while Bella looked on.

Priest holding his stance at the altar, Bible open, ready to continue.

Bridesmaids and groomsmen standing still, probably due to Taylor threatening them if they uttered a word or took a step off the line.

She met her sisters' gazes. They nodded. Order had been restored.

Bella escorted the couple back front and center the exact moment the last lingering note of music trailed off.

The priest smiled and skipped over the question he'd already asked, smoothly transitioning to the most important part of the ceremony. "And now, repeat after me..."

The vows were recited.

And once again, Avery relished a rush of satisfaction knowing she'd managed to provide the happy-ever-after her job required.

About Jennifer Probst

Jennifer Probst wrote her first book at twelve years old. She bound it in a folder, read it to her classmates, and hasn't stopped writing since. She holds a masters in English Literature and lives in the beautiful Hudson Valley in upstate New York. Her family keeps her active, stressed, joyous, and sad her house will never be truly clean. Her passions include horse racing, Scrabble, rescue dogs, Italian food, and wine—not necessarily in that order.

She is the New York Times, USA Today, and Wall Street Journal bestselling author of over 50 books in contemporary romance fiction. She was thrilled her book, The Marriage Bargain, spent 26 weeks on the New York Times. Her work has been translated in over a dozen countries, sold over a million copies, and was dubbed a "romance phenom" by Kirkus Reviews. She is also a proud three-time RITA finalist.

She loves hearing from readers. Visit her website for updates on new releases, and get a free book at www.jenniferprobst.com.

Discover 1001 Dark Nights

Jennifer Probst ~ BLOOD NIGHT by Heather Graham ~ TWIST OF
FATE by Jill Shalvis ~ MORE THAN PLEASURE YOU by Shayla Black
~ WONDER WITH ME by Kristen Proby ~ THE DARKEST
ASSASSIN by Gena Showalter

GRAVESIDE BAR AND GRILL by Darynda Jones ~ THE ANTI-FAN AND THE IDOL by Rachel Van Dyken ~ CHARMED BY YOU by J. Kenner ~ DESCEND TO DARKNESS by Heather Graham~ BOND OF PASSION by Larissa Ione ~ JUST WHAT I NEEDED by Kylie Scott

Discover Blue Box Press

TAME ME by J. Kenner ~ TEMPT ME by J. Kenner ~ DAMIEN by J. Kenner ~ TEASE ME by J. Kenner ~ REAPER by Larissa Ione ~ THE SURRENDER GATE by Christopher Rice ~ SERVICING THE TARGET by Cherise Sinclair ~ THE LAKE OF LEARNING by Steve Berry and M.J. Rose ~ THE MUSEUM OF MYSTERIES by Steve Berry and M.J. Rose ~ TEASE ME by J. Kenner ~ FROM BLOOD AND ASH by Jennifer L. Armentrout ~ QUEEN MOVE by Kennedy Ryan ~ THE HOUSE OF LONG AGO by Steve Berry and M.J. Rose ~ THE BUTTERFLY ROOM by Lucinda Riley ~ A KINGDOM OF FLESH AND FIRE by Jennifer L. Armentrout ~ THE LAST TIARA by M.J. Rose ~ THE CROWN OF GILDED BONES by Jennifer L. Armentrout ~ THE MISSING SISTER by Lucinda Riley ~ THE END OF FOREVER by Steve Berry and M.J. Rose ~ THE STEAL by C. W. Gortner and M.J. Rose ~ CHASING SERENITY by Kristen Ashley ~ A SHADOW IN THE EMBER by Jennifer L. Armentrout ~ THE BAIT by C.W. Gortner and M.J. Rose ~ THE FASHION ORPHANS by Randy Susan Meyers and M.J. Rose ~ TAKING THE LEAP by Kristen Ashley ~ SAPPHIRE SUNSET by Christopher Rice writing C. Travis Rice ~ THE WAR OF TWO QUEENS by Jennifer L. Armentrout ~ THE MURDERS AT FLEAT HOUSE by Lucinda Riley ~ THE HEIST by C.W. Gortner and M.J. Rose ~ SAPPHIRE SPRING by Christopher Rice writing as C. Travis Rice ~ MAKING THE MATCH by Kristen Ashley ~ A LIGHT IN THE FLAME by Jennifer L.

On Behalf of 1001 Dark Nights,

Liz Berry, M.J. Rose, and Jillian Stein would like to thank ~

Steve Berry
Doug Scofield
Benjamin Stein
Kim Guidroz
Chelle Olson
Tanaka Kangara
Asha Hossain
Chris Graham
Jessica Saunders
Stacey Tardif
Dylan Stockton
Kate Boggs
Richard Blake
and Simon Lipskar

Made in the USA
Columbia, SC
02 November 2023

25089771R00083